SEA GLASS FROM THE PAST

BLUE HERON COTTAGES
BOOK EIGHT

KAY CORRELL

ZURA LU PUBLISHING LLC

ABOUT THIS BOOK

Rose is poised at the beginning of a new chapter of her life. She's ready for a fresh start and a place to call her own.

But just when she thinks her life is settling down, secrets are revealed that shatter everything she's believed about her life.

And what about Aspen and Willow? They stand at a crossroads. Their inheritance remains a puzzle, and their father's fate, an unsolved mystery. Will answers finally come to light?

Enjoy this book full of long-held secrets, deep-rooted friendships, and the heartwarming spirit of a close-knit community. Join Rose and her friends as they find love, healing, and a few surprises in the conclusion of the feel-good Blue Heron Cottages series.

This book is dedicated to my family. To the crazy, boisterous times, the endless laughter, and the quiet moments together. I could never do this without all of you. You bring me such joy.

KAY'S BOOKS

Find more information on all my books at
kaycorrell.com
Buy direct from Kay's Shop at
shop.kaycorrell.com

COMFORT CROSSING ~ THE SERIES

The Wedding in the Grove - (a crossover short story between series - with Josephine and Paul from The Letter.)

LIGHTHOUSE POINT ~ THE SERIES
Wish Upon a Shell - Book One
Wedding on the Beach - Book Two
Love at the Lighthouse - Book Three
Cottage near the Point - Book Four
Return to the Island - Book Five
Bungalow by the Bay - Book Six
Christmas Comes to Lighthouse Point - Book Seven

CHARMING INN ~ Return to Lighthouse Point
One Simple Wish - Book One
Two of a Kind - Book Two
Three Little Things - Book Three
Four Short Weeks - Book Four
Five Years or So - Book Five
Six Hours Away - Book Six
Charming Christmas - Book Seven

SWEET RIVER ~ THE SERIES
A Dream to Believe in - Book One
A Memory to Cherish - Book Two

A Song to Remember - Book Three
A Time to Forgive - Book Four
A Summer of Secrets - Book Five
A Moment in the Moonlight - Book Six

MOONBEAM BAY ~ THE SERIES
The Parker Women - Book One
The Parker Cafe - Book Two
A Heather Parker Original - Book Three
The Parker Family Secret - Book Four
Grace Parker's Peach Pie - Book Five
The Perks of Being a Parker - Book Six

BLUE HERON COTTAGES ~ THE SERIES
Memories of the Beach - Book One
Walks along the Shore - Book Two
Bookshop near the Coast - Book Three
Restaurant on the Wharf - Book Four
Lilacs by the Sea - Book Five
Flower Shop on Magnolia - Book Six
Christmas by the Bay - Book Seven
Sea Glass from the Past - Book Eight

WIND CHIME BEACH ~ A stand-alone novel

INDIGO BAY ~

Sweet Days by the Bay - Kay's Complete Collection of stories in the Indigo Bay series

Sign up for my newsletter at my website *kaycorrell.com* to make sure you don't miss any new releases or sales.

CHAPTER 1

Rose sat on the beach watching the sunset, taking in the serenity of the moment. She now had a pair of comfortable wooden chairs that George had found and placed in her favorite spot on the edge of the beach. He'd turned out to be a pretty handy neighbor.

Not that he was actually her neighbor. She was staying at Violet's Blue Heron Cottages Resort yet again. She'd just returned to Moonbeam this afternoon following an emotional trip back home. But things were going to change. For real this time.

A soft breeze blew in from the gulf this evening, ruffling her hair. She pulled her wrap around her shoulders against the slight chill.

George came around the line of Areca palms, and his face split into a wide smile as he waved to her. "You're back. Great to see you again. Mind if I join you?"

A swell of warmth filled her at his friendly greeting. "I'd love the company."

He ambled over and sank into the chair beside her, stretching out his long legs. He'd tanned up quite a bit since he'd moved to Moonbeam, and his cheeks were ruddy from the wind and the sun. Life here seemed to agree with him.

He leaned back in his chair. "It's nice to have you back in Moonbeam. Missed our little chats when you were back home."

And yet, it hadn't really felt like home. "I missed Moonbeam more than I expected."

"How was your trip? Are you doing okay?" His eyes were filled with compassion.

"I'm doing okay. I think. It was difficult. I'm just glad to be back."

They sat in a comfortable silence for a few minutes, watching the sun dip lower over the water.

"Want to hear something that might cheer you up?" George finally said, an excited glint in his eyes. "I unpacked my very last box today. I'm fully moved in now!"

Rose laughed, her sadness dissipating. "That's wonderful! I bet that feels so good to be done."

"It really does," George said, leaning back in his chair. "Like I can finally breathe again... Like I'm home."

Home. Something she no longer had. She no longer felt like the house she'd lived in with Emmett was where she belonged, and she couldn't live in the peach cottage at Violet's forever.

She knew what she had to do—what she was going to do—she just hadn't told anyone her decision yet. The secret that had been simmering inside for weeks, months. It was just... if she said it out loud it would be true. It would be what her life would become. And it was such a huge change.

"What are you thinking about? I can almost hear the wheels in your brain spinning." George's eyebrow raised inquiringly.

"I was thinking—" She paused and looked at him. Who better to tell her decision to first? He'd understand. He'd been through it himself when he lost his wife, Becky. Yet her heart skittered at the thought of saying it aloud. Saying the actual words. She took a deep breath. "I wanted to tell you something. I've made a decision."

He shifted in his chair to face her. "I'm all ears."

Her heart pounded. It was time to say the words out loud. "I'm selling my house back home. I've decided..." She took a deep breath. "I've decided to move to Moonbeam."

His eyes crinkled with his wide smile. "Ah, I bet it feels nice to have made the decision."

"It does. I feel like I can't move on with my life if I stay in that house. And I've made so many friends here. Violet, Aspen, and so many people."

"Hope you consider me your friend."

She smiled at him. "I do. A good friend. You've been the perfect person to talk to while I figure out this stage of my life. You understand. You've been through it."

He nodded. "I have. And it's not easy. But I'm really glad I sold Becky's and my home and moved here. I feel like... like I can breathe again. That maybe the pain won't stab quite so deeply."

"I'd like that. I'd like to think of Emmett

and our good memories without the pain swelling over me, drowning me. And I feel like something is pulling me to move here. Maybe a push from Emmett. I don't know. That probably sounds silly."

"No, it doesn't. I sometimes can still feel Becky, hear her voice. I still talk to her." George shrugged. "So it's not so silly to feel like maybe he's pushing you to move here. Maybe he wants you to have that new start, too."

"Maybe. It's just a very strange, strong sense that I'm supposed to move here."

"So, I guess you'll be looking for a house?"

"Yes, I want a little beach cottage." She smiled. "And I'm betting Violet will help me paint it some cheerful color."

George laughed, glancing over at the brightly colored cottages of the resort. "I bet she will. I'll help too. With anything you need. Would you..." He paused, his brows drawing together. "Do you want help packing up your house?"

She shook her head. "No... I packed up most of it while I was back home. It's just something I needed to do on my own."

"I understand. It's hard to box up all those memories."

5

"I did manage to give away most of his clothes when I was back there this fall. Then the rest I gave away this last trip. And most of our furniture is old... and as much as I love it all... it might be nice to have new things. Lighter furniture more fitting for a beach home. So I also donated most of that."

"I bet you can find just the right things for your new place."

"I hope so." She swallowed. So many changes. Even if they were changes she was sure she needed to make.

George frowned. "So... what's wrong? You have this look on your face. Aren't you pleased with your decision?"

"I am. It's just... so... final."

"Taking that first step toward a new life. A different life. It's hard. A life we didn't expect to be living, did we?"

"No, I never imagined my life without Emmett in it." She put on a brave smile. "But, it's the right thing to do. And along with a bit of fear about all the changes, I'm kind of excited. You know, I've never lived on my own. I went from my father's house to living with Emmett after we married."

"I had my own apartment before Becky and

I got married, but it was still hard to learn to live on my own again after she died. I'm adjusting now, though. I think moving here to Moonbeam helped. Everything is new. And I didn't have any family to move closer to. I'm afraid I'm the last one standing from both our families." He looked over at her. "Do you have family?"

"No." She closed her eyes. "Well, yes. I do. I think I do."

"You think you do?"

"I have a sister. Had a sister. I mean, I don't know if she's still alive. We had a… falling out, I guess you'd call it. A huge one. I… I cut her out of my life. I could no longer trust her."

"I'm sorry." His eyes shone with sympathy. "That must have been hard."

"It was. We were really close growing up. Did everything together. Shared each other's clothes, had the same friends. She was only eleven months younger than me. And I couldn't believe it when she…" She closed her eyes again.

"That's okay. You don't have to explain. I can tell it's still painful."

"It is. You'd think I would get over it. Deal with it and leave it in the past. But… I obviously haven't." She sighed. "We were so close. You know that connection people talk about that twins have? We weren't twins, but we had that same kind of connection. I swear I knew what she was thinking. We'd finish each other's sentences. I could feel when she was near." She shrugged. "But, of course, I haven't felt that in years."

"You miss her?"

"I miss the sisters we used to be. Until we weren't... I've tried a few times to find her. Maybe see if we could be some kind of family again. As I've grown older, I realize that when we're young, we sometimes make mistakes. Grave mistakes. They change the course of our lives. Though to be honest, I have no idea what I'd do if I saw her again. If the anger and hurt would still be there." She still, after all these years, dreamed about that night and the last time she'd seen Pauline.

"Perhaps you should try again. Maybe you could find some peace if you did."

"Maybe. But right now I have enough changes going on. I'm going to look for a home here in Moonbeam. My house back home went on the market this week. I already have two offers. One is a cash deal and they want to close in two weeks."

"That's great. And I meant what I said. I'll help you in any way I can. I'll always appreciate your kindness when you introduced me to people here in Moonbeam when I first arrived. Helped me unpack my new house. I... well, I'd love to return the favor."

She smiled at him. "Thank you. I'll remember that." She leaned toward George. "And thank you for always listening. Being there for me. I really appreciate it."

He smiled gently. "Anytime. That's what friends are for."

Friends. Now that her secret was out, she couldn't wait to have coffee with Violet in the morning and tell her friend the news.

CHAPTER 2

"What?" Violet hurried out from behind the reception desk and threw her arms around Rose. "You're moving here to Moonbeam? For real?"

"I am." Rose hugged her back. "I made the decision a little while ago, but just wasn't quite ready to… to talk about it. I needed some time to adjust to the idea."

"Well, I think it is a fabulous idea. Wonderful. The best idea ever." Violet couldn't keep from grinning. She tugged on her friend's hand. "Come on, let's grab our coffee and go sit out on the porch. I've missed you. And tell me everything."

They settled into two chairs on the porch, and Violet leaned back. This was one of her favorite times of the day. Having coffee with Rose. Chatting about everything and nothing. And now, they could do this whenever they wanted. Perfect. This was perfect.

"It was a lovely sunrise this morning," Rose said as she blew on her hot coffee before taking a sip. "It reflected in the clouds over the gulf. Just beautiful."

"So you're staying here for our sunrises?" Violet teased.

"And so much more." Rose leaned back in her chair. "I need a change or I'll never move on. Emmett wouldn't have wanted me to just stop living my life, either. And I love it here in Moonbeam. I've made so many good friends. And really, who would I drink my coffee with if I moved away?" Her eyes twinkled.

"Now we can still have coffee all the time. I love that you're moving here. Love it. Oh, we should find you a place to live. I'll help you fix it up."

"I thought I'd ask Evelyn for the name of a Realtor."

"Oh, good idea. Those Parker women know everyone."

"I'd like to find a little place on the beach.

12

Where I can sit out and watch the waves, the birds, the sunsets."

"We'll find you the perfect place. I just know it."

Violet couldn't believe how much had changed in her life since she'd made the rash decision to buy the rundown Murphy's Resort, restore the cottages, and make the place her own. Now it was Blue Heron Cottages. Her brother, Robbie, hadn't been happy with her decision, but he'd come around. Especially since he'd married Evelyn, and he'd never have met Evelyn if she hadn't bought the cottages.

"Did Danny get back to Moonbeam yet?" Rose's question interrupted her thoughts.

Danny. That was another big change. "He should be here soon. He and Allison went back to Tallahassee to pack up their house. They found one here and should be moving in the next week, I believe. I can't wait to have them living here, too." She grinned again in pure happiness. "All my favorite people are going to be here."

"Who knew you'd find love right out of the blue at Christmas?"

"I certainly wasn't expecting it. Wasn't

looking for it. But Danny is just the best guy ever."

"He is nice. I'm happy for you two. And Allison. His daughter seems really happy to be moving here."

"Didn't hurt to find out that they're related to our Moonbeam Parkers." Violet paused, her brows drawn. "I sometimes think Moonbeam is... I don't know... magical. It has a way of healing people. Of bringing people together."

"I know it's been good to me. I plan on having a happy life here once I find a place of my own."

Violet grinned again. "Did I mention how excited I am that you're moving here?"

"Maybe once." Rose's eyes twinkled as she picked up her coffee, raising the mug slightly. "To many, many more mornings just like this one."

Within days, the Realtor Evelyn suggested had taken Rose to see a dozen houses. None of them seemed right to her. Maybe she was being too picky. But it seemed so important to find the perfect house this first time living on her own.

The first house she'd own all alone. A couple houses were too dark. A few needed way too many repairs. One should have been perfect, but she just didn't feel like it was supposed to be hers. Silly, she knew. But that's how she felt. And she tried to always go with her gut feelings.

Luckily Emmett had invested well, and she had a nice little nest egg, plenty of money to buy a cottage. They'd lived frugally all their years, so a cottage on the beach seemed like such an extravagance. But it was something she wanted to indulge herself with.

If she could find the right home.

She got up from the couch at the sound of a knock on her cottage door. She opened the door to find George standing there grinning. "Hey, I have some news."

She smiled at his enthusiasm. "And this news would be?"

"I just saw my neighbors. The ones on the other side of me. Guess what? They're moving. Putting their house on the market next week. It's in the price range of the homes you've been looking at. They said you could come see it now if you want."

"Now?"

"It's cute from the outside. Haven't been in.

They said it's two bedrooms, two baths. So not very large. They do have a wonderful, big deck overlooking the gulf."

"I'd love to see it."

"Well, come on then. Let's walk over there."

She and George walked down the beach. An older couple waved to them from the house next to George's. They climbed up the stairs of the deck, and the woman reached out and took Rose's hand. "George says you're looking to move here. I admit, I'm having a hard time letting go of the house. We've lived here for ten years. But, now we want to move back closer to our grandchildren."

"You certainly have a wonderful view from your deck." The deck was spacious, with plenty of room for chairs and a table.

"I will miss the view," the woman said. "Jim and I have really loved living here. We're actually leaving tomorrow. Selling the house furnished except for my kitchen things. I still want all my kitchen equipment and dishes. But we're moving into a small one-bedroom condo, so we don't need all this furniture. Oh, and I should introduce myself. I'm Helen, and this is my husband, Jim."

"It's nice to meet you."

Helen motioned to the door. "Come inside."

She and George followed the couple inside. Rose gasped in delight when she saw the main open area. Sunlight streamed in the windows, dancing around the room. The couch was a tropical print that somehow managed to not look too loud or gaudy. Off-white easy chairs sat next to it, and a white-washed coffee table set off the sitting area.

The kitchen was recently remodeled with light maple cabinets and shiny new appliances. A farmhouse sink was centered under a large window.

"Your home is beautiful." She turned to Helen.

"Thank you. I'll miss it for sure."

She followed Helen back to see the nice-sized primary bedroom with a large, airy bathroom. Then the extra bedroom was a good-sized room, too, with a second full bathroom in the hallway.

She couldn't imagine a more perfect house. There was just something about it. Like the house itself knew it would become her home. They all stepped out onto the large deck and she took in the view again.

She turned to Helen and Jim. "I love your house." Should she buy it? Was this the one?

Her blue heron friend swooped in for a landing and stood at the water's edge, staring at her, as if telling her that this was her house.

And she knew for certain. This was the right house. It pulled at her. Opened its arms to her.

She turned to the couple. "I love the house. Everything about it. How light it is. The kitchen is wonderful. And this deck? It's perfect. George told me the asking price, and I think it's very fair. I would like to buy the cottage. I can pay cash so we could close quickly."

Tears sprang to Helen's eyes. "Oh, I'd been hoping we could sell to someone who will appreciate it like we did."

Jim wrapped his arm around his wife's shoulder. "I told you it would all work out. Someone would love the house as much as we did." He turned to Rose. "I'll have our lawyer draw up the paperwork and send it to you. I think this is all done online now."

"That's perfect. I'll leave you my information so the lawyers can work out the details."

"I feel so much better leaving tomorrow, knowing this is all settled." Helen brushed away a tear. "I feel like this house was meant to be yours."

Somehow the fact that Helen felt that way made her own feelings about the house deciding it was hers seem less strange.

She and George left Helen and Jim's house —soon to be her house. She turned to George. "Do you mind if we take a little walk? I'm just so... happy. And jittery. And surprised it all went so quickly."

"I could see your eyes light up when you walked inside. It's a beautiful cottage."

"It is. Did you see the light yellow walls in the main bedroom? I love them. So cheery. And the furnishings are just what I would have picked out."

"Looks like we're going to be neighbors then." George nodded as they headed down to the water.

"It does look that way." She lightly rested her hand on his arm as they walked along the uneven sand until they got to the hard-packed sand by the water's edge. The blue heron stalked ahead of them, watching.

She sucked in a deep breath of the fresh air, then spun around to look back at the cottage. It was painted a weathered teal color with white trim. And it was hers. Or it would be. It was the perfect shade of teal. Her favorite shade with just a bit more green than blue to it.

Pauline used to tease her about her pickiness about the color teal. Which shades of it she loved. Which ones she said weren't really teal.

Now, where had that thought come from? But Pauline had been on her mind the last few days. Ever since talking about her with George.

"You okay?" George stood with his feet just barely in the water, letting the gentle waves lap against him.

"I am. I'm just a bit overwhelmed right now. I mean, I made the decision, but now it's... real."

"It is real. You're going to own your first home that you bought yourself."

She let out a long sigh. "I guess I'm going to head back home and schedule movers for the few things I'm bringing with me. My kitchen things since Helen said she's taking those. And I have a few pieces of furniture that I can't part with. I'll bring those and see if I can make it all work."

"I'll be happy to have you as my neighbor." George smiled at her.

Excitement raced through her. She was

moving. Into her own home. A perfect cottage with lots of light and painted the perfect color. She laughed out loud. "I feel like I could twirl around like a young girl I'm so happy." She flung her arms out wide.

"Don't let me stop you." He grinned.

She spun around once, feeling silly. But then spun around again. "That felt good." She reached down and splashed at a wave. "I'm finally going to feel like I have a home again."

The heron paused and looked at her, dropped his head slightly as if in agreement, then took off, swooping into the sky.

She placed her hand to block the sun and watched as the bird disappeared into the distance.

CHAPTER 3

A few weeks later, Rose stood in the front room of her old house. The movers had come and gone. She'd packed up her clothes, her kitchen items, and a couple of small pieces of furniture. Her car was loaded with things she didn't trust to the movers. A few pieces of jewelry Emmett had bought her. Nothing fancy, but she treasured them. A painting of a beach scene they'd found at a street fair years ago. A box of breakable keepsakes she wanted to make sure made it to Moonbeam intact. And lastly, one of Emmett's favorite sweaters she couldn't bear to part with.

The only thing missing was her favorite piece of sea glass. She didn't know where it had gotten to. She and Emmett had found it on a beach walk on their honeymoon at Murphy's resort. She always kept it in the milk glass bowl on their dresser. But it wasn't there when she went to pack up her things.

She still hoped it turned up somewhere in some box or the other. It kind of broke her heart to think it might be missing. She shoved the thought aside, taped up the last box, and stood looking around the room.

The thunderous silence engulfed her. No music playing while she cooked dinner for Emmett. No sound of Emmett reading bits of the newspaper to her or whistling as he puttered around the house.

Just… silence.

Now just a void where before so much life had existed, all wrapped up in the cocoon of this house.

She slowly walked to the kitchen, footsteps echoing, and opened the familiar back door. Stepping onto the porch, a sob caught in her throat. How many hours had she and Emmett spent out here over the years? So many mornings sipping coffee and planning their days. So many evenings holding hands and watching the sunset, then the stars.

The porch sat stark and bare now. She'd

given away the two chairs they'd had out here. She'd briefly thought about moving them to Moonbeam, but then Emmett's chair would always be sitting empty, reminding her he was gone.

The bird feeder in the yard stood vacant, reproaching her, not a bird in sight. Guilt crept through her. Maybe she should have filled it with seeds one more time. The new owners had been delighted there was a bird feeder, so hopefully they'd fill it right away for her little friends. She'd miss sitting out and watching the birds.

While she felt she'd made the right decision to sell the house, leaving still pierced her heart. It was hard to leave it behind and close the door on all the memories.

The couple that bought the house were thrilled to be moving in. She hoped they loved it as much as she had. That they'd fill it with their own joy, their own memories.

She went back inside, locking the door behind her. One more walk around the house. She slowly moved into each room for one last look. One last glance out the living room window overlooking the backyard. She straightened the curtains—would the new owners even want them? They'd likely paint and update everything until it was their own. Change everything.

She blinked, chasing away tears. But life was full of changes. Nothing ever stayed the same. And it was time for her to make changes, too.

She was ready. At least, she thought she was. Not that she could alter the plans she'd put into motion now.

She stood in the doorway, telling herself it was time to leave. "Goodbye, house. You were very good to us. Be good to the new owners." She paused, her hand on the doorknob. "And Emmett, I know you'll still be with me wherever I am."

With a deep breath, she pulled the door closed behind her for the final time.

CHAPTER 4

Violet looked up as Aspen burst into the office at Blue Heron Cottages late in the afternoon, her cheeks flushed. "Is Willow here yet? I got tied up on my shift at Jimmy's and couldn't get away." She bent over and took a deep breath. "Practically ran the entire way here."

"She's here. All tucked into the yellow cottage."

"I can't believe she's here for a week." Aspen's voice bubbled with excitement.

"Your sister had a big binder with her and said it was chock full of wedding ideas. She's really excited to be here to help you plan your wedding."

"Awesome. I'm going to head to her cottage

now." Aspen paused at the door. "If you don't need me here in the office?"

"No, we're good. I made a smart decision to hire Deanna to help us if I do say so myself. There's so much to do during the busy season, and she's a hard worker."

"She's nice, too, isn't she? I like her. And it is crazy busy here in Moonbeam in the winter. We're just slammed at Jimmy's all the time. Lunch and dinner."

"With more help here at the cottages, you can help out more at Jimmy's." Violet smiled. "And see Walker more, of course."

Aspen glanced down at the sparkling diamond on her finger. "I still can't believe it. I'm engaged. I'm getting married."

"And I'm thrilled for you." Violet came out from behind the desk and walked over to the door. "And it was so thoughtful that Walker arranged for your sister to be here when he proposed to you at Christmas, wasn't it?"

"It was." Aspen furrowed her brow. "So much happened last year. Finding out I have a sister. Falling in love with Walker. Getting engaged."

Violet laughed. "Not sure how you'll top that this year."

"Well, there is the wedding." Aspen's brown eyes sparkled with excitement. "That's going to be pretty special."

"It certainly will be."

"I'm so glad Willow came to help me plan it. I don't know anything about weddings, really."

"Well, you're sure going to find out now." Violet gave her a little shove out the door. "Now, go. Deanna and I have the front desk covered. You just have fun with Willow this week."

Aspen turned and hurried across the courtyard to her sister's cottage. The door flew open, and the women embraced. Violet smiled as she walked back inside. She couldn't be happier for Aspen. She hoped Aspen had a wonderful week with her sister and got all her wedding plans made. Aspen's life had taken a magical turn filled with good fortune. Yes, she firmly believed, Moonbeam did have a way of sorting out the lives of people who came here.

Aspen threw herself into Willow's welcoming embrace. "Willow, you made it."

"I told you I would." Willow stepped back,

grinning. "It's not every day I get the chance to help plan my sister's wedding."

Aspen followed Willow into the cottage. "Violet said you showed up with a big notebook full of plans."

Willow nodded toward the table where a large blue binder sat spread open wide. "I have so many ideas."

"It looks like you do." Aspen looked at the three-inch binder brimming with pages. It was a good thing one of them knew something about planning weddings.

"Don't worry," her sister assured her. "We'll make it the perfect wedding for you. Whatever you want."

Aspen sank into a chair at the table. "I'm not sure what I want. Something simple. And I'd like to have it here at the cottages. Violet offered to let me have it here for free. I tried to tell her I needed to pay something, but she insisted. Said I was family. But I guess that's good because I don't have much saved up for the wedding."

"I can help with expenses." Willow sat down across from her.

"No, I don't want that. I need to do it on my own. Well, Walker is helping with expenses too.

I just don't want it all to be on him. I need to do my part."

"I have an idea on how to keep expenses down…" Willow jumped up from the table. "I'll be right back."

She returned holding a garment bag. "Now you don't have to say yes, but I thought I'd offer." She unzipped the bag and pulled out a white dress with delicate lace trim.

"Oh, that's beautiful."

"It was mine. We could have it altered to fit."

Aspen went over and took the dress, holding it up to herself. "It's exactly what I would have picked."

"Then—but only if you're sure it's what you want—the wedding dress is figured out."

"Oh, I'm sure. I love it. Really."

"Go try it on."

Aspen went into the bedroom and slipped on the dress. It was a little tight in the waist, so it would need to be let out a bit there. The bust was a bit too loose, so that would have to be adjusted, too. But overall, it was perfect. And just what she would have chosen for herself if she'd really thought about her wedding dress. Which she should have been doing. She really was a rookie with this whole wedding thing.

She hurried out to show Willow. "What do you think?" She spun around slowly.

"I think you look beautiful."

Aspen laughed. "Right, with my hair in a braid from work and bare feet."

Willow's lips curved into a smile. "I've always wanted a sister to share clothes with."

"I think I'm getting the better end of that. My clothes are... well, not as nice as yours."

Willow hugged her. "But it's more than just the clothes. It's... having a sister. I sometimes still can't believe it's true."

"I can't either. And I can't believe Magnolia kept this secret from us for all those years."

"It does hurt to think Mom just gave me up for adoption like that. But my adopted folks were great."

Aspen scowled. "Yeah, I think you got the better deal there. Having Magnolia for a parent was not the best thing to ever happen to me. She was a terrible mother."

Willow touched her hand. "I'm so sorry you had such a rough life growing up. But I'm so happy that things are working out for you now."

"I feel like I need to pinch myself to make

sure I'm not dreaming." She looked down at her engagement ring again. "I'm just so... happy."

"You deserve to be happy. And Walker is lucky to have you."

She blushed at the compliment. "I should go take this dress off before I spill something on it or wreck it."

She changed out of the dress, hanging it up carefully in Willow's closet, then headed back out to sit at the table. She slipped into the chair by her sister. "Not to change the subject from weddings, but has Derek's detective found out anything more about Dad?"

"He's still working on it." Willow sighed. "Wouldn't it be perfect if we could find him?"

"We don't even know if he's alive. Maybe he's, uh, dead like Magnolia." It still shocked her to think of her mother as dead. Magnolia was always full of life... and herself... and it seemed impossible that she was gone. Not that she'd seen her mother for years. Not since Magnolia had disappeared and left her alone right before her high school graduation.

"No, I refuse to believe that. I want him to be alive. I want to meet him. Magnolia stole you from me, and Dad from me. And I just..."

Willow shrugged. "I want to get the chance to meet him."

"Don't get your hopes up too much. It's been a very long time. And Magnolia didn't give us much to go on."

"We'll find him. You'll see." Willow's eyes flashed with determination.

She wasn't as certain as her sister but didn't want to smash Willow's hopes. And really, Willow had gotten everything she needed and wanted in life. Great parents after she'd been adopted. A wonderful home. College. And marrying Derek. And they had the cutest, healthiest son. A charmed life, really.

She couldn't help but be the tiniest bit jealous. But she was glad that Willow had a chance for a better life than she had. She wouldn't wish her childhood and early adulthood years on anyone.

She pushed the thoughts aside, concentrating on the present. "Oh, and I ran into the lawyer, Mr. Brown, the other day. He says that Magnolia's money is still all tied up in the legal system. I still can't believe she left us millions. I mean, Magnolia never had any money. Ever. And I'm not surprised that her dead husband's kids think she tricked him out of his money. I wouldn't be surprised if she did."

"It does seem strange to think of inheriting that kind of money from a woman who gave me away." Willow shrugged. "I guess we'll either get the money or not."

The money probably didn't mean much to Willow. She and Derek had tons of money. She could tell by the clothes Willow wore and the pictures of their home. While she had barely saved enough to help cover some of the costs of the wedding. She and Willow were as different as night and day. Kind of like a modern-day princess and the pauper. And unfortunately, she was the pauper.

Willow reached over and touched her hand. "I'm sorry. I know the money would change everything about your life."

"I certainly could use the money, but I'm not really sure how I feel about taking it if the judge does decide it's ours. All I wanted from Magnolia was... her to love me. Spend time with me. At the very least, not just taking off and leaving me for days or weeks at a time. I was just a kid. Who does that?"

"I don't know. I don't understand it.

Especially now that I have Eli." Willow shook her head.

"Anyway, I have everything I want. Everything I need. I found out I have a fabulous sister." She grinned. "And now I'm marrying Walker. What more could a woman want?"

"Maybe to have her wedding all planned?" Willow laughed. "Do you want to see the wedding planner I brought?"

Aspen grinned. "Yes, all three inches of pages."

CHAPTER 5

Violet frowned at the computer, perplexed. Something wasn't adding up. She'd hate to have to ask Robbie to come look at the books again. She was certain she had turned a profit this month, but the numbers on the screen seemed to tell a different story. They had to be lying to her.

She glanced over at the windows that looked decidedly naked without all the Christmas lights and decorations she'd put up in them during the holidays. Maybe she shouldn't have spent all that money. But she loved having all the festive decorations up. And she'd left some white twinkle lights up in the courtyard, so there was that.

Concentrating on the screen again, she

stared at the numbers. A slow grin spread across her face as she realized her error. "Ah, ha. There you are." She changed an expense she'd duplicated and hit refresh and there it was. A profit. A small profit, but a profit nonetheless.

She heard the crunch of the crushed shell drive as someone pulled up outside and paused her input on the computer. No one was due to check in this afternoon. The door swung open and her mouth curved into a delighted smile. "Danny." She rushed across the room and he gathered her into his arms.

"Mmm, you feel so good," he murmured. "So good. I've missed you."

"I've missed you too." She looked up, taking in his shining eyes and warm smile. "I thought you weren't coming until next week."

"Finished up the packing. Movers came. So Alli and I decided to head out here. I dropped her off at Sea Glass Cafe. She wanted to see Emily. I'm sure she's going to try to see if she can get a shift tonight. She's missed working there."

"Oh, but I thought your home wasn't ready until next week."

"It's not. But I checked online, and it looks like you have an opening in the pink cottage.

How about it? Does that work for us to stay here until the house is ready?"

"Yes, that works for me. Works very nicely." She hugged him again, happiness bubbling through her at his unexpected early arrival. "Come on, I'll get your keys."

"Okay, in just a minute." He tugged on her hand, pulling her back. "First, I need a kiss."

She grinned up at him. "I think that could be arranged."

He kissed her and the world faded away as she got lost in his kiss, his arms. When he finally released her, she stood there, clearing her thoughts, bringing herself back to the real world.

"You keep doing that and I'm liable to forget what I was doing," she admitted with a dazed shake of her head.

"The keys." He nodded toward the desk, grinning at her.

"Right, that's what I was doing." She went over and grabbed the keys to the pink cottage. "Here you go. One for you, one for Allison."

"Thanks. I'm going to unload my truck, but then maybe we could sit out on the porch if you're not too busy?"

"I'm never too busy to spend time with you."

"Perfect. I'll be back in a few." Danny disappeared out the door.

Violet went to the owner's suite attached to the office and grabbed a handful of the local craft beer that Danny loved. She iced up a bucket and plunged the bottles in. She glanced in the fridge and didn't see much she could feed him. An apple to slice, and some cheese and crackers. That would have to do.

She carried it all out to the porch just as Danny appeared again. "What's all this?"

"I thought you might be hungry." She teased. "You're always hungry."

"I'm a growing boy."

"Pretty sure you haven't been a boy in a very long time." She sat down on the loveseat on the porch.

Danny settled beside her and slipped an arm around her shoulder. She leaned back, content. She was right where she wanted to be.

"So tell me all the news," Danny said as he opened two beers and handed her one.

"Not much has been going on here. There's going to be a big gala at The Cabot Hotel. Oh, and the Jenkins twins went on a vacation for two weeks, so no new gossip since they left."

His answering chuckle touched her heart. "We'll have to see if we can give them something to gossip about when they return."

"And Willow is here visiting Aspen. They're going to plan Aspen's wedding." She set her beer down quickly. "Oh, oh. And how could I have forgotten to tell you the biggest news? Rose is moving to Moonbeam."

"Wow, she is? That's great."

Violet let out a contented sigh. "It is great. I'll have everyone I love here with me in Moonbeam."

Danny winked at her. "Everyone you love?"

She laughed. "Yes, everyone I love. You, Allison, Robbie, Rose. So many people. And all the Parkers who have basically decided I'm part of their family."

"Lucky I'm part of that family, too." Danny leaned over and kissed her again. "I'm so glad to be back."

"And soon we'll get you all moved into your new house."

"I checked on my phone and it's a ten-minute walk from the cottages."

"That far?" She grinned at him.

"I could jog. That would make it quicker."

"Oh, Danny. I just never thought my life would turn out like this." Joy swept through her. Contentment. A sense that everything was falling into place.

He swept a lock of her hair away from her face. "And I never thought my life would be as wonderful as this, either. Funny how love can find you when you least expect it."

CHAPTER 6

A spen and Willow walked into Beach Blooms the next morning, the sweet floral scent washing over them as they entered.

"Good morning, ladies." Daisy, the owner, greeted them. "Are you here to start planning those wedding flowers?"

"We are. My sister's in town helping me plan."

"And today is picking out the flowers," Willow added.

"Do you have anything specific in mind?" Daisy asked.

"I'm not sure…" Aspen ran her gaze around the shop. There were so many flowers and so many choices. She was completely overwhelmed.

"Roses?" Willow suggested.

"No, too formal for me." Aspen shook her head. "I want something... simple."

"Depending on the wedding date, we could do some white ranunculus blooms, white dahlias, or maybe peonies."

Aspen sighed. "We don't have a date yet. Walker wants it to be soon."

"So this summer?" Daisy pursed her lips. "I think we could pull off a very pretty bouquet of mixed white flowers with some lavender. Oh, or maybe blue with it. Possibly some delphinium or blue thistle? Maybe some eucalyptus? Simple, but very pretty."

"That sounds lovely." Willow turned and looked at her. "Does that sound good to you?"

"I guess so. I'm not sure I even know all those flowers."

Daisy laughed. "I forget not everyone knows flowers like I do. Here, let me show you some examples."

Daisy pointed out the different blooms around the shop, then showed her photos of more choices of white flowers. After some discussion, Aspen felt more confident in the floral choices. Daisy chose a pale blue ribbon to complement the flowers perfectly.

"The bridesmaids could wear blue dresses," Willow suggested.

"Sure." Aspen tried desperately not to feel overwhelmed. Bridesmaid dresses. That decision needed to be made, too. "But I was just going to have you as the matron of honor. And Walker is having his sister Tara for his best—I don't know —best person?"

"Perfect, we'll look for a dress for me this week, too." Willow scribbled something on the pad of paper she was carrying.

"I could do a smaller bouquet of similar flowers for Willow then. Maybe with a splash of blue flowers with small white ones?"

Aspen nodded.

"And we'll need some flowers for the reception table." Willow glanced at the small pad again. "Then a boutonniere for Walker and we'll have to figure out something for Tara."

Daisy nodded, continuing to add notes about reception flowers and boutonnieres as Aspen's head spun. She was so grateful to have Willow here managing all the planning details.

Daisy wrote up the order, and Aspen promised to get back to her on the actual wedding date as soon as possible. She and Willow headed back outside.

"Now what?" Aspen knew her sister would have the day planned.

"Now we're going to go to..." Willow consulted her list. "Barbara's Boutique. Violet gave me the name of the shop. We'll see if she has a dress for me to wear. And we'll need shoes."

"Don't you just have a dress that might work? I hate for you to spend money."

"Nonsense. Part of wedding fun is picking out dresses. I thought we'd try Barbara's, but if we can't find a dress there, we can go into some of the bridal shops in Sarasota."

An hour later, they walked out of Barbara's Boutique with a knee-length dress for Willow in a rich baby blue color. Willow triumphantly crossed bridesmaid dress off her list. "Now we're going to go eat."

Of course, her sister would have planned their lunch, too. She probably had every detail of the week planned out. But at least at the end of the week, the wedding would be planned.

"I thought we'd go to Jimmy's. I haven't seen Walker yet. Or are you tired of Jimmy's since you work there?"

"No, Jimmy's is fine." Familiar. Not strange, like this whole wedding planning thing.

They put Willow's dress in the car and headed to the wharf. Tara greeted them at the entrance. "Aspen, Willow." She hugged Willow. "I heard you were coming to town to help plan the wedding. Maybe you can convince these two to pick an actual wedding date."

Soon they were seated at a table with a view of the harbor. Walker waved to them from where he was working behind the bar.

After a few minutes, he came over and hugged Willow. "Good to see you. I didn't know you two were coming in today."

"Hey, Walker. Good to see you, too. Couldn't miss having a meal at Jimmy's."

He leaned over and kissed Aspen lightly on the cheek, his eyes shining with delight at seeing her. Yes, Jimmy's was familiar. Walker was familiar. She started to relax. Just a nice break from the planning.

"So, how about picking a wedding date?" Willow asked.

Or not a break.

"I'd marry her tomorrow if she'd agree to it." Walker's mouth curved into an infectious grin. "But then, my mother would kill me if we didn't have a proper wedding."

"So? Any ideas when you want to do it?" Willow would not let them avoid it.

"Um... next September?" Aspen looked at Walker.

"How about sooner?" Walker nudged her. "This summer?"

"How about June?" Willow suggested.

"It's going to be hot and humid then. And if we're having it outside at the cottages, there's always a good chance of rain then." Aspen frowned.

"We could get a tent set up in the courtyard. Then you wouldn't have to worry about the weather and it would give us shade. Or we could see about having it at The Cabot Hotel. They have the pavilion," Walker suggested helpfully.

"I'd really like to have it at Violet's."

"Then Violet's it is." Walker squeezed her hand. "Anything you want."

She looked at him gratefully. "Okay... June would work."

Walker broke into a wide grin. "Perfect. I might be able to wait that long." He winked at her.

"Which weekend?" Willow asked, taking out her phone and pulling up the calendar.

"First one?" Walker asked.

Aspen couldn't resist his enthusiasm. "Yes, that works if it works for Violet."

"Here, I'll call her." Willow got up and walked away to the edge of the restaurant to call her.

"You doing okay?" Walker asked. "You look a bit... dazed."

"There's just so much that's involved in planning a wedding. I guess I never really thought about it. Didn't think I'd ever get married."

"And yet, here we are." He kissed her lightly on the top of her head. "Planning a wedding."

"I just want it to be... simple. I'm not sure Willow's version of simple and mine are quite the same."

"We'll make sure you have exactly the wedding you want. I promise."

Willow came back. "We're on. First Saturday in June." She slipped back into her seat.

"Perfect. And now that the date is picked, Tara will quit nagging me." He laughed. "Okay, I need to get back to work. I'll see you later."

Walker headed back behind the bar and

Willow pulled out her pad of paper, checking yet another thing off her list. Wedding date. Check.

Willow looked up at Aspen and furrowed her brow. "What is it?"

"I'm just… I'm just worried. It's probably silly to worry about, but Walker knows half the town. He has a huge family. His side of the wedding is going to be packed with people, and I'll have… you, Violet, and Rose. The most lopsided wedding ever."

"We don't have to do bride and groom sides with the seating. And you know a lot of people in town now, too."

"But all of them knew Walker first." Walker didn't exactly understand her reservations, her worries, she knew that. And she'd feel silly trying to explain this to him.

"It will be okay. I promise." Willow scribbled a note.

"I don't know how you know how to do all this." Aspen shook her head.

"Do what?"

"Plan a wedding. Figure out all that needs to be done."

"Well, I planned my wedding. I've been a

maid of honor at a few weddings and helped plan them."

"It all seems so foreign to me."

"Don't worry, I'll help you with everything."

But it still seemed like a lot to do before the first week of June...

CHAPTER 7

Rose looked around the peach cottage. She'd spent last night here, waiting for closing on her new house. It had all gone well, and she had the key now. She grabbed her overnight bag and looked around the cottage. So many memories here, too. From the first time she and Emmett had stayed here on their wedding night, to the annual trips back here to celebrate their anniversary. But now it was time to say goodbye to this cottage too. At least staying here. Because now she had her own home here in Moonbeam.

Violet came to the door. "You all set?"

"I am. I think. It's just been a couple of hard days of saying goodbye."

Violet walked in and hugged her close. "I know it has. Lots of changes."

Rose stepped back. "I'll be fine."

"I know you will." Violet nodded vigorously. "And you'll love your new house. And I'll love having you here in town."

They walked out onto the porch. "I guess it's time to head over to my new house."

"I wish I could go with you, but Deanna's not here yet."

"I'll be fine." Rose figured if she kept saying that enough times, maybe she'd believe it.

Violet waved to her as she pulled away, out the drive, and onto the street. Of course, it was only moments until she reached her home. It was so close. She got out of her car and looked at the cottage. She did love the paint color. It had a cute, welcoming front porch with white railings. A poinciana tree adorned the corner of the front yard.

She took a deep breath, climbed the front steps, and unlocked the door. Her hand shook slightly, which annoyed her. Excitement or nerves? She opened the door and stepped inside, her heart scurrying in her chest. She took a few more steps and broke into a grin. Her home.

Sunlight poured through the windows,

welcoming her. She crossed the main room and looked out toward the water with the waves rolling constantly to shore. She threw the doors to the deck open wide. Salty air filled her lungs as she walked out onto the deck and took a deep breath. Yes, this was the perfect home for this stage of life.

She walked back inside and slid the screen closed on the door. Glancing at her watch, she wondered when the movers would be here. Supposed to be sometime this morning.

"Rose?"

She turned to see Violet standing in the front doorway.

"Come in." She hurried to greet Violet.

"Deanna showed up and I couldn't wait any longer to see your house." Violet handed her a large vase of brightly colored flowers. "A little welcoming present. Didn't know if you'd have a vase, or be able to find one, so I stuck them in an antique mason jar I had lying around."

"Thank you. They're lovely." She set them on a narrow table along one wall, glad to have the company of her friend for this first exciting day in her new home.

"Oh, and here. My favorite coffee. So you can make some in the morning. Though, really,

I'd prefer you to just keep coming to the cottages for coffee." Violet grinned.

"I'll still come over a lot, I'm sure."

"So, are you excited?"

She nodded. "Excited. A bit nervous. I can't wait to get my things moved in."

"I could help you unload your car while you wait for the movers."

"I'd love that."

They unloaded the car, stacking the boxes in the corners, out of the way of the movers. Violet headed into the kitchen to wash the shelves, and Rose went to unpack a suitcase of clothes she'd brought with her.

Violet came into the bedroom a short time later. "I've got to run. Get back to work. But call me if you need anything. I gave Aspen the week off, but I can still get Deanna to cover the desk if I need to."

"I'll be fine." There were those words again. "Thank you for your help."

Soon the movers arrived, and the house was full of men hauling in boxes while she directed where to put them.

It didn't take them that long to unload her things, and she signed the paperwork and they were gone.

Suddenly, she was in her new house. With the things she'd brought. It was all very, very real. And different. But somehow it felt like she belonged here. Like the house wanted her here. She was supposed to be here. A very comforting feeling.

She went into the kitchen and started putting away her things. First, her set of white dishes. Then the collection of mismatched coffee cups. But she loved each one for the memories they held. She and Emmett used to buy them on their trips. She carefully unwrapped each one and placed it in the cabinet. She filled the pantry, the cupboards, the drawers. After an hour or so, the kitchen was all unpacked. Progress.

She really should tackle the bedroom next, but she was running out of energy. Maybe tomorrow.

A glance around the kitchen as she tried to figure out what she could make to eat made it clear that she really needed to grocery shop.

A knock came from the front door, and she walked over to answer it. George stood in the doorway and held up two paper bags. "I thought you might like something to eat. I picked up sandwiches from Sea Glass Cafe."

"Oh, you're a lifesaver. I was just trying to figure out if I had anything to eat at all."

"I got a sandwich for me, too, if you don't mind the company."

"I'd love it. Come in."

Rose got out some plates and George unpacked their meals. She got them both water and wished she'd thought to make tea earlier.

"So, are you doing okay?" He sat down across from her at the kitchen table.

"I'm fine." If she said that one more time, she was going to scream. But she was fine, wasn't she?

"It will take some time to adjust. I'm just now feeling like my cottage is home, that Moonbeam is home."

"I kind of already feel like this is home. It's... strange. Like I've lived here before or something, though of course I haven't."

"Well, that will make it easier to feel settled, won't it?"

She nodded. "I hope so."

As they ate, George regaled her with a story of the Jenkins twins' newest gossip. He laughed. "They've only been home two days and already know everything that's happened while they were gone. They knew about you moving into your new house today and said to tell you congratulations."

"That was sweet of them."

"And they knew that Danny and Allison plan to move into their house this week. Plus, I'm pretty sure they'll be finagling for an invitation over here to see your place soon."

"Oh, I need to get all unpacked and settled in before people can come over."

"I'm here." He winked at her.

"That's different. You and Violet... you're good friends."

"That's what I like to hear." He smiled and reached for a piece of peach pie.

CHAPTER 8

Aspen and Willow strolled along the water's edge that evening, arm in arm. "It was a productive day," Willow said. "We got so many decisions finalized."

"Like when the wedding is going to be. Are you sure we can have everything ready in time?" Aspen thought there was way too much to do before then.

"Don't worry. I promise everything will be perfect. Tomorrow we'll decide on invitations." Willow frowned. "Unless you think Walker will want to help make that decision?"

"I... I don't know. Maybe?" She shrugged. "I'll ask him when I talk to him tonight."

"Good idea. Oh, and Violet gave me the name of someone over on Belle Island who can alter the wedding dress. Ruby. I called and set up an appointment with her this week."

The overwhelm started to take over again. "Um... okay." Just how many appointments did one have to make when planning a wedding?

"Oh, and the minister? Do you have someone picked out to marry you?"

"The pastor from Walker's family's church. Walker already checked, and he's good with our wedding date."

"Perfect." Willow laughed. "I should have brought my list with me so I could check things off."

Or they could just not talk about the wedding plans for a little bit...

Willow's phone rang, and she glanced at the number. "I'm sorry. Do you mind if I get this? It's Derek. We've been missing each other's calls."

"No, go ahead. I'll just walk a bit down the beach. Do some shelling." Get a break from the planning. Though she didn't mean to think ungrateful thoughts. She was very appreciative of the help. Was it wrong to just want the wedding to be over? To be married to Walker? To just be in that stage of life with all this behind her? She must not be normal. Didn't women dream about their wedding for years? About how they wanted it to be? Every little detail?

As she walked along, something caught her eye at the edge of the waves. The waves retreated, and she reached down and scooped up a piece of sea glass. So pretty in a pale mint color. She wondered what this piece of glass used to be part of. A jar? A bottle? An old window?

"Aspen. Wait up." Willow hurried down the beach toward her. "You'll never guess what Derek said."

"What?"

"He has a lead on Dad."

Aspen's heart somersaulted in a triple beat and she grabbed Willow's hand. "Really?"

"The best lead he's had. I mean, nothing is for sure, of course. Other leads have fallen through."

Aspen tried to keep her hopes from getting out of hand.

"How wonderful if we could actually find him. I have no memories of him at all." Willow looked out at the water, then turned back. "You're lucky to have known him. Have some memories."

"I don't have many. I remember him taking me for an ice cream cone once. The ice cream fell out of the cone and I started crying. He laughed and bought me another one. And I remember being at a park with him. On the swings. He was pushing me and I felt like I was flying." It had been a long time since those memories had pushed into her consciousness.

"Anything else?"

"I remember... " She frowned. "I remember his hands. They were big and always warm. He'd hold my hand as we walked down the sidewalk. I thought he was so tall." She laughed. "But who knows, since I was so young then. Everyone was tall."

"I wish I would have known him. Had any memory of him at all."

"I have a memory for you." Aspen reached out and took Willow's hand. "You were a baby. It was the middle of the night and you were crying. I got out of bed to check on you. Magnolia would just let you cry. She always said you'd cry it out. But Dad must have gotten home that night from one of his business trips. I walked into your room and he was sitting in the rocking chair, rocking you, singing you a lullaby."

Willow's eyes filled with tears. "Really?"

"I'd forgotten all about that night until we started talking about him."

"He pulled me up on his lap and rocked both of us. I guess I fell asleep because the next morning I was back in my bed. And woke up to Magnolia yelling at him. Then he slammed out of the house that morning. I think that might be the last time I saw him."

"Maybe we'll get the chance to see him again."

"Maybe. I hope so. How long until Derek will know more?"

"The investigator is checking it out. Maybe in a few days? Unless..." Willow's eyes filled with sadness. "Unless it's a false lead and I never get the chance to meet him."

"Don't think like that." She squeezed Willow's hand. Though she wasn't going to get her own hopes up too much. She'd had enough disappointments in life. She didn't need another one. Although she had to admit, her life sure had turned around in the last few months.

She tugged on her sister's hand. "Come on. I just found some sea glass. Let's see if we can find any more."

～

Aspen opened the door to her cottage later that evening and grinned when she saw Walker standing there. "I didn't know you were coming by tonight."

He stepped inside and pulled her into his arms. "I couldn't wait any longer to see you. To kiss you." He kissed her gently, pulling her close to him.

For a moment, all the wedding plans and stress melted away.

He stepped back. "So, did you get a lot of things settled for the wedding today?"

Or maybe not. Maybe it would be all wedding all the time until they finally got married. "We did. Made a lot of decisions. Picked out flowers. And Aspen found a dress."

"That's good." He took her hand and led her over to the couch. "Tell me more. Everything."

"It's... a lot. So many decisions." She settled against his side.

"I guess that comes with the wedding territory. I'll help in any way I can."

"Thanks. Do you want to help pick out the wedding invitations tomorrow?"

"If you want me to."

She laughed. "I... I don't know. I don't even have a strong opinion on them. I feel like I'm failing in the bride department."

"Don't be silly. You're doing fine."

"I just... I just want to be married."

"Well, I would have suggested we elope, except for the fact that my mom would have killed us."

"And Willow. And Violet." She sighed. "No, I want the wedding to be nice. And I am looking forward to it. There's just so many details and decisions."

"We'll get through it. I promise." He took her hand and squeezed it.

"And... and you'll think this is silly, but at the wedding..."

"What?" He frowned.

"All the town is going to be sitting on your side. Like every chair filled. And I'll have like a couple of people on my side."

"We won't have sides."

"But people expect it."

"We don't have to do what people expect. Besides, the whole town loves you. We can make up signs. Aspen and Walker's side and Aspen and Walker's side." He grinned at her.

She laughed. "That might work."

"And it's not silly. You can worry about any detail you want to worry about and I'll try to fix it for you. I want this day to be exactly what you want."

Was he not the most perfect man ever? She looked up at him. "Have I told you lately how much I love you?"

"You love me?" He widened his eyes. "Why, I didn't know that. Tell me all the ways."

"I love that you're always here for me. That you listen to me. That you want to spend your life with me."

"And I do." He pulled her close. "We're going to have a beautiful life together."

And Aspen didn't doubt that for even a moment. They would have a beautiful life. She just needed to pinch herself to believe it was real. And hers for the taking.

CHAPTER 9

Rose carried an opened box of books over to the shelves in the main room. She'd gotten rid of a lot of her books when she moved but still kept way too many. Her favorite novels that she loved to reread. A handful of cookbooks. Some of Emmett's favorite books, too. She just couldn't part with them. His complete collection of Sherlock Holmes that he must have read at least fifty times. She promised herself she'd only keep the ones that would fit on this one bookcase. Maybe. It had been hard enough to part with the ones she'd already given away.

She reached into the box and pulled out a handful of her old favorites, carefully lining them up on the shelves. Fiction on a couple of shelves. The cookbooks all together on another shelf. And then Emmett's books.

The doorbell rang, and she slid the thick Sherlock Holmes collection onto the shelf and went to answer it.

She opened the door, and a woman stood there with a tentative look on her face. "Um... hi."

"Hello, may I help you?"

"I'm looking for Rose. Rose Sherman."

She smiled at the woman. "I'm Rose."

The woman stared at her intensely for a moment. "Oh... uh... good." Relief swept over the woman's face. "I was afraid I wouldn't find you. I went to your old address. When I found out you moved, I was afraid... I was afraid I wouldn't be able to..."

"What is it?" Rose frowned.

"Your old neighbor told me where you'd moved, thank goodness." The woman pulled herself up straight, her gaze lingering on Rose's face before reaching into her purse. "I have something I'm supposed to give to you."

"You do? What is it?"

"This." The woman held out a letter.

Rose glanced at the letter and gasped. She

slumped against the doorframe when she saw the handwriting. Emmett's. "But how?"

"He sent it to me. Told me to give it to you after he was gone. But to wait a bit. Give you some time to… adjust. Then, when I decided it was time to give it to you, I was afraid I wouldn't find you."

"I don't get it. How do you know Emmett?"

"I think you should read the letter. He'll explain."

"Okay, why don't you come inside?" Rose stepped back to let the woman enter. The woman gave her the letter and Rose stared at it, her hand trembling.

"You should open it. It will explain everything. Emmett thought it was time you knew… well… read the letter."

Swallowing hard, she opened the letter, as her heart pounded riotously in her chest. She drew in a deep breath and unfolded the pages.

My dearest Rose,

I miss you already and I'm not yet gone. I know you'll get this letter right when you need it. I'm hoping you're doing fine. That you're moving on with your life. I want the remainder of your life to be filled with happiness.

So I decided you need to know this. I made a promise years ago to keep a secret, and I've kept it. But I'm gone now, so... it's time you knew the truth.

I know this will come as a shock, and I'm sorry about that. But you should know I've kept in contact with Pauline over the years. And I've helped her out some. Given her some money. You see, I found out Pauline was pregnant. And your father kicked her out of the house. I don't know many details or who the father was, but he wasn't around helping her.

I was certain if you knew about it, you'd want to help her even if you were still angry with her. And you'd want to help the baby. But Pauline made me promise not to tell you.

Maybe I should have broken that promise and told you, but as the years went by, it seemed harder and harder to explain why I'd kept Pauline's secret. And you know how I am about promises. I don't break them. I'm so sorry. It is the only secret I've ever kept from you. I swear.

And now I'm going to try and make it right. It's right for you to know this now. I'm going to make sure you get this letter after I'm gone. And I think you should reach out to Pauline. I hope you two can find your way back to each other. Give her a chance to explain why she

*did what she did. You need family with you now. So...
I've sent you some.*

*I'll always be with you, but please move on with
your life and seize what happiness you can.*

All my love,

Emmett

PS - Your niece's name is Emma Rose

She sank onto the couch, holding the letter
against her chest. Emmett had been in contact
with Pauline? He'd given her money? He'd
helped her? Even after what she'd done?

Anger surged through her. And hurt. He'd
kept this secret from her all these years. She
never would've believed he would keep
something like this from her. Ever. How
could he?

And just as quickly, the anger softened.
Because Emmett's words were right. Even after
what Pauline had done, she would have never
turned her away if she'd known Pauline was

pregnant. If she'd known their father had thrown Pauline out.

And her father hadn't said a word about any of this when she'd sat by his bedside when he was dying. He'd chased both his daughters away. Did he have any regrets?

All these thoughts rumbled through her mind. So many things that she thought she knew, that she was certain of, just disintegrated into dust.

She looked up at the woman standing beside the couch, watching her. She frowned. "But why did Emmett send this letter to you?"

"Because... I'm Emma Rose. Your niece. My mother named me after the two of you. Emma for Emmett, and Rose for you. Everyone calls me Em."

"You're Pauline's daughter?" As if the letter hadn't been shocking enough. She stared at the woman, seeing a faint resemblance to Pauline in her features.

"I am." Em stood there staring at her, uncertainty hovering in her eyes.

Rose got up from the couch and placed the letter on the coffee table, then walked over to Em. "Oh, my... my goodness." Her words stuck in her throat. Tears gathered in her eyes. "I don't know what to say. I have a niece. You're my niece?"

Em smiled tentatively. "Yes, I am."

"Does Pauline know you came here?"

"No, I didn't tell her. Emmett told me that it would have to be up to you whether you reached out to Mom or not. But he said I had the right to meet you and get to know you. I don't know what happened between you and Mom, but... I really hope you'll reach out to her and maybe we can all be a family."

Rose's thoughts whirled around. She could find Pauline now if she wanted to. Emmett had made that possible. But did she want to? Would they be able to work things out? *Did she even want that?*

"I met Emmett a couple of times, you know."

"You did?" Yet more surprises. How many more did this day have in store for her?

"He was in town on business a few times and he had dinner with us. He seemed like such a great man."

"He was."

"Anyway, I was hoping... I mean, I hope it's okay if you and I get to know each other. Do you think that would be okay?"

"Of course it would." She had a niece. Family.

"I got a room at The Cabot Hotel. I was planning on staying for a few days before heading back to Savannah, if that's okay with you. That's where Mom and I live." Em frowned. "Or maybe you need some time to get used to all of this."

"I do need some time. But please don't leave town. I…" Her thoughts were still spinning and her world tilted dangerously off-kilter. So many changes all at once. She cleared her throat. "Would you like to come back tomorrow? After I have a little time to sit with all of this."

"Of course."

"Come by at lunchtime. We'll chat and get to know each other."

"I'd love that," Em said eagerly. She headed to the door, then turned and paused. "And Rose?"

"Yes?"

"I'm really, really glad to finally get a chance to meet you." Em smiled and slipped out the door.

Rose walked over and sank onto the couch again, then picked up the letter and read it over and over. Everything in her life had changed with this letter. Everything.

"Oh, Emmett. Why didn't you tell me? We could have worked something out. And you're right. I would have helped Pauline. Even after what she did."

Em walked into The Cabot Hotel and looked up at the grand chandelier. The lobby was sparkling with light and polished wood. Okay, she'd chosen right. This looked like a fabulous place to stay.

She rolled her bag up to the reception desk. "Welcome to the Cabot." The woman behind the desk greeted her.

"Hi. Your hotel is beautiful."

"Thank you. It's just recently been renovated. There's a history room off the lobby if you would like to see some old photos of how it used to look."

"Thank you. I'll do that."

"And we've upgraded you to a suite. No extra charge."

"Oh, wow. Thank you." This did seem to be

her lucky day. She'd actually tracked down Rose and now she got a suite?

"Mr. Hamilton—he owns the hotel—likes to randomly upgrade guests. It's a lovely two-bedroom suite. I'm sure you'll enjoy it."

"Tell him thank you for me." She reached for the offered key.

She headed up to her top-floor room and opened the door. Light flooded the room through the large doors leading out to a balcony. Yes, she would enjoy staying here a few days. She smiled as she crossed the room, opened the French doors, and stepped outside.

The salty sea breeze ruffled her hair. The sun sparkled off the water in the harbor. A large sailboat sliced across the bay. A fishing boat bobbed near some pilings sticking out of the water near the edge. They must have held up a pier at one time. Maybe an errant hurricane had taken it out.

She let out a long, deep breath. Stress had been her constant companion the last week or so. First deciding it was time to deliver the letter to Rose, only to find out she had moved. Then finally finding her down here in Moonbeam. Not to mention telling her mother she was away on business. A little white lie remedied by stopping by a client's on the way here.

Rose looked a lot like her mother. It was easy to see they were sisters. They had the same eyes and facial features. But where Rose had lovely gray hair, her mother had brown hair, carefully dyed. Even their voices sounded the same.

For about the thousandth time, she wondered what had happened between Rose and her mom that had caused them to cut each other out of their lives. Emmett had never said a word about it on his visits. Her mother refused to talk about it. But at least Emmett was trying. He'd sent the letter for her to give to Rose. And she had. Her part was finished. Well, kind of. She still hoped to convince Rose to contact her sister. Maybe they could work things out. Maybe.

Her stomach rumbled, reminding her she hadn't eaten since early morning. She hurried back inside and peeked at both bedrooms before choosing the largest, sunniest one. She pulled her suitcase into the room. A king-sized bed sat against one long wall across from a bank of windows overlooking the harbor. An overstuffed chair sat by the window as if beckoning a guest to sit down and read. She quickly unpacked, carefully hanging up her clothes and putting her toiletries in the large bathroom.

She ran a brush through her hair and put on some fresh lipstick. That was good enough. With one last glance around the suite, she headed down to the lobby.

The elevator smoothly glided to the first floor with a tiny bump as the floor number flashed above the door. She walked to the concierge desk. "I'd like a place to grab a casual lunch."

"Sure." The man pulled out a printed page with a map of Moonbeam. "Here's the wharf and there are quite a few restaurants there. Jimmy's on the Wharf is great. Or Brewster's. And then there is Sea Glass Cafe. Right downtown. You can walk to any of these if you like."

"Thank you. I think I will."

She headed outside and paused at the wide expanse of the drive looping up to the main door. A fountain splashed cheerfully out front.

With one more look at the map, she headed downtown. Sea Glass Cafe it was.

Rose sat outside, watching the sunset, sipping a glass of wine. She must have read the letter a dozen times. Tracing the words with her finger. Emmett.

She still couldn't believe he'd kept this secret all these years. She would have sworn they never had a secret between them. But she guessed it was Pauline's secret to tell. But she so wished he'd never promised Pauline that he'd keep her secret.

And it was so like Emmett to help Pauline out. He was so kind. So generous.

"You look lost in thought." George stood at the top of the stairs to the deck, interrupting her musings.

"I... I am."

"Do you want to be left alone?" His forehead crinkled. "Are you okay?"

"I'm fine." She shook her head. No use in pretending. "No, I'm not. I'm not fine at all."

"Do you feel like talking?"

"I guess so. I'm just so... confused. Come. Sit. I'll grab you a drink and you can join me. Beer? Wine?"

"I'll have what you're having."

She disappeared inside and returned with a glass of wine. He'd settled on the chair beside hers and she handed him the drink. She sank back onto her chair, wondering where to start.

As usual, he gave her time. Gave her space.

"I don't really know where to start."

"The beginning is always a good place." He gave her a gentle smile.

She took a deep breath. "So... I found out so many things I didn't know today."

"Like what?"

"Like I have a niece. She was actually here. And my sister is alive. She lives in Savannah."

"How did you find all this out?"

"From Emmett."

George's eyes widened. "From Emmett?"

"He... he wrote a letter that he wanted me to get after he was gone. It's a long story, but he's been helping out my sister and my niece. Been in contact with them."

"Wow. I don't know what to say."

"I don't either. I can't believe that Emmett kept this secret. It... it hurts."

"I'm sure it does," George said softly.

"But I kind of understand why he did. Pauline made him promise. And really, it was Pauline's to tell that she had a child." She frowned. "I wonder who Em's father is."

"Em? That's your niece?"

"Yes, Emma Rose. Pauline named her after Emmett and after me." She leaned forward, staring out at the sea. "Why would she do that when I cut her out of my life?"

"Maybe she still cared about you. Wanted the connection to you."

"Maybe." She sighed. "It's all so much to take in."

"Are you going to see your sister? Contact her?"

"I... I haven't decided. But Em is coming over here tomorrow for lunch. I... I can't believe I have a niece I knew nothing about."

"It will be nice to get to know her, won't it?"

"Yes, I think it will. I mean, nothing that happened between Pauline and I had anything to do with Em. But Em never got to know me all these years since Pauline and I... well, we didn't speak."

"Maybe it's time you two did talk."

"It's been so long. But I still don't know how I'll feel if I see her. It's been over forty years."

"Only you can make that decision. Decide if you want to reach out."

"Wow, I knew it would be a big change when I moved here to Moonbeam, but I had no idea just how much my life would change."

They sat there in silence while the sky darkened and the stars began to pop out in the distance, blinking slowly in the heavens.

"George?"

"Hm?"

"Thanks for listening. You really are a good friend."

"Glad I could be here for you."

CHAPTER 10

"I can't believe how much we got done this week." Aspen set down her cup on their table at Brewster's where she and Willow had come for breakfast.

"I told you we'd knock out the list." Willow had her ever-present list on the table.

"You're like a master at all of this. I would have never been able to get all this done without you."

"And didn't you just adore Ruby? She was so sweet. And she said she'd have your dress done soon and you could go back for another fitting."

"She was really nice. And she said she can make it work. I don't know though. You are so... thin. And I'm... not."

"Yes, you are. And you're beautiful. And

Walker adores you. And you're going to have the best wedding ever."

"The first weekend in June." Aspen grinned. "My wedding planner made me pick a date."

"Hey, Walker is the one who can't wait to be married to you." Willow shoved back her plate with the remains of a peach croissant still resting on it.

Aspen had eaten every single crumb of her own croissant. She eyed what was left of Willow's but refused to ask for it. This is why Willow looked like she did. She could actually leave part of that delicious pastry.

"So, I talked to Derek this morning. And I have some bad news…"

"What is it? It's about Dad, isn't it?"

"It is. Turns out the lead didn't pan out. Another dead end." Willow sighed. "I'm afraid we're never going to find him."

"Don't give up hope. Maybe something will come up."

"Maybe." Willow looked at her watch. "We should probably head over to the lawyer's office. We're supposed to meet up with him in twenty minutes."

Aspen scowled. "More drama about the inheritance, I'm sure. And honestly, if Magnolia did scam her—what did the lawyer say—*fourth* husband? Then I don't want the money. His kids deserve it. And Magnolia might not even have been legally married to him since our lawyer can't find any divorce decree between her and Dad."

"Well, let's go see what Mr. Brown has to say."

They paid their bill and got up, then walked down the wharf and into the parking lot. They headed down the sidewalk and got to the lawyer's office right on time.

"Ms. Caldwell, Mrs. Sampson. Good to see you. Come in, come in." The lawyer stood and motioned to two wooden chairs across from his desk. "Glad you could come.

"And Ms. Caldwell, I understand congratulations are in order. You're getting married. I ran into the Jenkins twins the other day and they told me."

"Yes, Willow has been in town this week helping me plan everything."

"Good. Good."

"So, you have news?" Willow asked as she glided into her chair. Aspen wasn't sure how Willow could make every single movement look so graceful. She settled on her own chair and grimaced as her purse slid off her shoulder and banged to the floor.

Mr. Brown sat back down, suddenly all business. "Yes. As you know, Magnolia's husband's children are contesting the will. Even though Magnolia left quite the hefty sum to each of you. Millions."

"But if she cheated him out of it, I don't blame his kids for trying to break the will." Aspen frowned. She didn't put it past Magnolia for marrying the man just to get his money.

"I'm doing my best to make sure you get the money your mother wanted you to have. But things are dragging on. It might take some time. And right now… it seems the man's children are at an advantage. And I still find no record of Magnolia's divorce from your father." The lawyer shuffled some papers.

"You haven't been able to locate our dad either, have you?" Willow's eyes held a hint of hope.

"Afraid not. Which is too bad. He might know how to locate that divorce decree. But I haven't given up."

"So you just wanted to meet with us to give us an update?" Aspen, as nonchalantly as possible, nudged her purse under her chair with her foot.

"Well, one of the man's children would like to meet with you. One of his daughters."

"Really? Why?"

"She didn't say. But she said it was important. It appears his three children are at odds over this whole legal battle."

"Really? That's interesting," Willow said.

"Funny how wills can sometimes bring out the worst in people." He shrugged. "But, I strongly suggest you don't contact them. It's not a smart move in a case like this."

"I wonder what she wants?" Aspen frowned.

"I don't know. But like I said, not a good idea."

"Okay, we'll go with what you suggest." Willow nodded, making the decision for both of them.

Mr. Brown stood. "Great. And if I hear anything more about the case, I'll be sure to let you know."

"Or if you find out anything about our father?" Willow shook Mr. Brown's hand.

"Yes. Certainly."

Aspen grabbed her purse from under the chair and hurried after Willow as she left the office. "What do you think all that was about? What do you think his daughter wants?"

"I really don't know. But I think we should take Mr. Brown's advice." Willow paused. "He knows best."

"I don't think it would hurt to hear her out."

"Maybe. But let's just do what Mr. Brown asks for now."

Aspen still couldn't see what the harm was, but she didn't want to argue with her sister. Not after she'd done so much for her. Helped her plan the wedding.

They stood out on the sidewalk, and Willow pulled out her list. "Okay, we still have a few more details to wrap up."

Of course they did.

CHAPTER 11

Rose got up early and headed to Sea Glass Cafe to pick up sandwiches and a salad for lunch. Then she stopped by Beach Blooms for flowers. Maybe a nice vase of flowers would camouflage the fact that her cottage was still a disaster of unpacked boxes.

"Rose, good morning," Daisy welcomed her to the shop.

"Hi, Daisy. Thought I'd pick up a nice, bright bouquet of flowers. I'm having... ah... company for lunch."

"Oh, lunch plans are always fun. I just got in a fresh batch of daisies, always my favorite." Daisy grinned. "I also have some lovely hibiscus. I could put some greenery in with them. They don't last long, but they are so pretty. Or a mixed bouquet."

Rose wandered over to the refrigeration unit and peeked through the glass. "How about that bouquet?" She pointed to one Daisy already had made up.

"Great choice." Daisy rang up the purchase and handed the flowers to her. "Have a nice lunch."

"Thanks, Daisy." She headed home and put the flowers in a pretty teal vase, one of her favorites. One that was her perfect shade of teal. She shook her head, still hearing Pauline's teasing words always accusing her that she had such strong opinions on the perfect shade of teal. Okay, she *did* have opinions on teal, and this shade was *perfect*. She put the vase on the kitchen table, then set the table, readying it for lunch.

She finished unpacking the box of books that she'd left when Em had shown up yesterday. Then she opened a box of throw pillows and a quilt she'd made and placed them on the overstuffed chairs. A touch of her own things. She found a box of photos and placed a few on the bookcase. An old photo from her and Emmett's wedding. One of Emmett sitting out on their porch, the warm light of the sunset casting a golden glow over him. She dug deeper in the box and spied a photo of her and Pauline. They must have been in their early twenties. Before everything fell apart. They were sitting on a blanket on the beach. It was taken the weekend they'd gotten married at Murphy's resort.

She debated putting it on the shelf but wasn't sure she was ready to see that photo every day. She wrapped it back up in the tissue paper and placed it back in the box. Leaning over, she scooted the box over to the corner, then stood up, stretching her back. The cottage was still a bit of a mess, but at least it looked a little more like hers.

Promptly at noon, she heard a knock at the door and went to answer it. Em stood there with a bouquet in her hands. "Hi, these are for you."

"Thank you." Rose took the flowers from her. "That was so thoughtful. Let me put them in water. Just take a seat. I'll be right back." She put the flowers in a vase and placed them on the center of the kitchen table, removing the ones she'd bought and placing those on the sideboard. She wanted to make sure Em knew her kind gesture was appreciated.

She returned to the main room and sat down across from Em. Silence hung between them.

"I thought—"

"I wondered—"

They both laughed.

"You go first." Rose motioned to Em.

"I was wondering why you moved to Moonbeam."

"Ah, you see. Emmett and I got married here at the resort. Just a few cottages down from here. We came back every year on our anniversary. After he died, I came back one last time. Or I thought it would be one last time. I ended up staying for a few months. And came back this winter for the holidays. Then, after going back home a few times, I decided that I could never move on in that house. It kept me stuck in the past."

"I could see how it might feel that way." Em nodded.

"And I've made new friends here. I thought it would be a good place to... to start over."

"It is a cute little town. I walked around this morning. There's even a general store here. So adorable. And I swear it has everything you'd possibly need."

"It sure does. And we have the lovely wharf with its restaurants and shops. And the people here are so friendly. I already feel like I belong here."

"That's really nice. Mom and I recently moved to Savannah. We escaped the harsh winters of Chicago. That's where we lived before Savannah."

"Chicago? I had no idea Pauline had moved there. So... what does Pauline do? For a job, I mean."

"When I was young, my mom worked as a nanny. Luckily, the family let her bring me with her. But then the kids she nannied got to school age and so was I. So Mom got different jobs. It was really hard then. We didn't have much money. Those were the years that Emmett helped us out. As soon as I was old enough, I started babysitting for extra money."

She still couldn't believe that Emmett had known all about Pauline. About Em. And never told her. The twinge of hurt niggled at her again.

"Eventually Mom worked her way up to a management job and things got better. I got a scholarship to college, then a good job after I graduated. Finally, things turned around for us.

I bought a small house, and it had a mother-in-law suite with it. Not that Mom was a mother-in-law, but she moved in there."

"That must have been nice for both of you. To live so close, but have your own space."

"It was. Then Mom retired, and we both got tired of Midwest winters and decided to move south. We settled on Savannah. We bought a duplex there."

"Do you like it there?"

"Pretty much. Doesn't really feel like home yet."

"And what do you do for a living?"

"I design websites and stuff like that. So I can basically live wherever I want."

"Oh, that's nice." She wanted to ask how Pauline was. Was she happy? What was she like now? But instead, an awkward silence fell between them again.

"Where does Pauline think you are now?"

"Visiting a client. I did briefly stop by a client's on my way here." Em smiled slightly. "I couldn't lie to Mom. But Emmett did say it had to be your choice on whether to see Mom. Do you think... do you think that you might reach out to her?"

"I honestly don't know. I did try to find her a few times, but didn't have much luck."

"But now you can. It will just take one phone call." Em's eyes filled with hope.

"I... I just need to think a bit more."

"I understand." Disappointment clouded out the hope. "You have to do what's right for you. Emmett made me promise it would be your decision."

So many promises made behind her back. She sighed. "I appreciate that."

"I did meet your father once." Em leaned back on the couch.

Shock skittered through her. "You did?"

"I was a teen. I was mad that Mom was working so hard and we just never had much at all. I found out my grandfather's name. And I snuck off to find him. He lived in that big old house. All alone."

"And how did that go?"

"I marched up and rang his doorbell. He answered the door. I knew it was him from a photo Mom had of the three of you."

"What did he say?"

"I told him that I was his granddaughter. His daughter's daughter." Em blinked back tears. "And he said that wasn't possible. He didn't have any daughters."

That sounded just like something her stubborn father would say. "I'm sorry, Em. Father was set in his ways. And if he thought Pauline or I weren't doing what he wanted us to do, he just quit being our father. He cut me off when I married Emmett. I guess he did the same with Pauline when she got pregnant with you."

"I know Mom wrote to him once after I was born. Sent him a baby picture. But she never heard back from him."

"My father was his own worst enemy."

"I just don't understand a family that cuts their family members out of their lives."

And there it was. Looming right there between them. Maybe she wasn't so much different than her father, after all. Because hadn't she cut Pauline out of her life, too?

But that was different. She didn't trust Pauline anymore.

"Can't you please at least try and talk to Mom? Try and work through whatever happened?" Em pleaded. "It would mean so much to me. To have you in my life. To have the three of us as a family. I've never had a family. Just Mom."

Rose nodded. "I won't make any promises, but let me think about it."

"Thanks, Rose." That hopeful expression spread across Em's face again.

CHAPTER 12

Aspen and Willow sat outside on Willow's porch on the last night of her stay. Willow had her ever-present list and pen on the table between them. Aspen admitted she'd had a great time with her sister, but she was ready to be finished with most of the wedding planning. Now she just hoped the wedding turned out perfect because Willow would be so disappointed if it didn't.

A car pulled up to the office, and a woman got out and disappeared into the office. "Hm, I thought all the cottages were filled this weekend. Wonder who that is." Aspen took a sip of wine. Willow had bought a bottle and said it was a nice red. Aspen didn't know much about red wine, but it did taste good. She almost choked when she saw the price of the bottle though.

A few minutes later Violet came walking out of the office with the woman and headed over to Willow's cottage. "Aspen, this woman is looking for you."

Aspen stood, having no clue who the woman was. The woman approached and held out her hand. "Hi, I'm Denise Wilkerson."

She paused, her hand in midair. Wilkerson. That was her mother's married name. Willow rose and stood beside her. "Are you Fred Wilkerson's daughter?"

"I am." She peered at Willow. "Are you Aspen's sister?"

Willow dipped her chin. "We're not supposed to talk to you." Willow threaded her arm around Aspen's waist in solidarity.

"I just... I know. My lawyer said the same thing. But... I have something for you. I thought you might like it." The woman held out a box.

Aspen reached for it, ignoring Willow's frown. "What is it?"

"It's a few of your mother's things. And there's a photo of her in there, too. I thought you'd want them."

Aspen opened the box and almost gasped

when she saw the photo of her mom. Magnolia had always been pretty and used it to her advantage, but she'd grown truly beautiful as she'd aged in that way that some women did.

Willow peeked over her shoulder and looked at the photo. "Oh, she's so beautiful."

"She was." The woman paused and looked at both of them. "And I know my siblings are all about cracking the will… But I don't agree with them."

"You don't?" Aspen eyed the woman.

"No, I don't. Magnolia was so good to our father. So kind. She stayed by his side the whole last year of his life while his health was failing."

"Magnolia did that?" Aspen could barely believe that. It sure didn't sound like the Magnolia she knew.

"She did. And the five years before that— they were married for about six years before Father died—they traveled around the world. Father was like a different man. Magnolia made him happy. I'm forever grateful to her."

"I should go and let you all talk." Violet stepped back. "You good?"

Aspen nodded. "We're fine."

Violet nodded and headed back across the courtyard.

Willow turned to Aspen, a questioning look in her eyes. Aspen nodded. "Denise, would you like to join us?"

"I would," the woman said eagerly.

Willow disappeared inside and returned with another glass. The three of them settled onto the chairs and an awkward silence fell between them.

Finally, Denise broke the silence. "My siblings… they think that Magnolia tricked Father. But I know the will is exactly what he wanted. He wanted to make sure Magnolia was taken care of after he was gone."

Aspen still couldn't picture her mother sticking around, taking care of a sick and dying man.

"I met Magnolia quite a few times. She and I talked for long hours, sitting beside Father's bedside toward the end. She said she had many regrets in her life. Made mistakes when she was young. She told me…" Denise paused and looked at both of them. "Told me how she put Willow up for adoption and how she was a lousy mother to you, Aspen."

"She said that?" Aspen picked up her wineglass and took a sip, then looked over the rim at Denise. What other surprises did she have in store? What other impossible-to-believe stories about Magnolia?

Denise nodded. "My siblings never came by to see Father the whole last year that he was dying. Didn't fly in even one time. I just didn't understand that. I came in as often as I could. Thank goodness Magnolia was there for him the whole time."

"I'm having a hard time picturing this Magnolia. Doesn't sound a bit like my mother." Aspen tried hard to reconcile the beautiful woman in the photo and the one who stayed by her husband's side with the woman who up and ran off and left her alone as a teen.

"Well, she was wonderful to my father. I came to the house the last morning and found Magnolia curled up in Father's bed with him, holding his hand. He died less than an hour later. Peaceful. Happy."

Aspen glanced over at Willow and saw tears in her eyes. But even after hearing how wonderful Magnolia was to Mr. Wilkerson, it didn't erase the anger she still had toward her mother.

"Anyway, I'm sorry about all the legal hassles my siblings are causing. I'm doing my best to make sure Father's wishes are upheld."

"It looks like Magnolia might not have been legally married to your father," Aspen said. Maybe she tricked Mr. Wilkerson into thinking they were actually married without bothering to get a divorce from her first husband.

"I don't care. She loved him. He loved her. She stayed by his side every step of the way of a very long, dark year."

"I'm glad she could be there for him," Willow said softly.

Aspen felt like Willow was betraying her, complimenting Magnolia on how nice she'd been taking care of her husband. Why hadn't Magnolia been able to take care of her own daughter?

"Anyway, I just wanted you to know all this. And know it's not every one of us fighting the will. I'm fine with you both getting all the inheritance."

"But really, I understand why your siblings would want it. It was your dad's money. And after Magnolia died, I'm sure they thought it should go to them." Aspen set down her glass. "And I don't want anything from Magnolia. Nothing at all."

Denise looked at her for a long moment. "I know Magnolia hurt you. She told me how she up and left right before you graduated high school."

"Did she tell you how she disappeared on me for days on end when I was younger than that? How I had to hide food in my room for times when she'd disappear? And that I was always afraid someone would find out she was gone and throw me into some kind of group home?" Aspen's anger spilled over. Denise was painting this picture of a kind, caring woman. And Magnolia wasn't that woman. She wasn't.

"She did say she was a horrible mother and was sorry. She said she tried her best, but that her best was... not good."

"No kidding," Aspen said, only halfway under her breath.

"I think giving you the money is her way of saying sorry. For how she raised you. And how she gave Willow up for adoption."

"Like money will fix any of that." Aspen stood and paced to the edge of the porch, leaning against the railing.

Denise stood. "I didn't mean to upset you. I just thought you'd like to have that box of her things and the photo. And I wanted you to know how good she was to my father."

Willow stood. "I thank you for coming and telling us. That was very kind of you."

"I'll go now. But here is my phone number. You can call if you want. If you have any questions. Or… for any reason." Denise handed a card to Willow and turned to Aspen. "Your mother really did regret the mom she was with you."

Aspen didn't care what her mother had said about regrets. Regrets didn't change things.

Denise turned and crossed the courtyard and drove away. Aspen stood at the railing, her thoughts whirling in her mind. She turned to face Willow. "I just can't picture *my* Magnolia as Denise's Magnolia."

"People change, you know. And it does sound like she was very sorry."

"Sorry doesn't make up for it."

Willow came over and placed a hand over hers. "No, it doesn't. But letting anger at Magnolia take over your life and eat on you. That doesn't help either."

Aspen snatched her hand away. "Gee, thanks for telling me how to feel. You don't understand. You had the perfect life. Ended up with wonderful parents. Had every advantage. Look at you. In your big house, with your wonderful husband and son. Your fancy clothes. Your perfect life. You don't understand anything."

Willow stepped back, her eyes wide and full of hurt. "I am sorry you had such a hard, terrible childhood. I am."

Aspen instantly regretted her words. "Willow, I'm sorry."

Willow just nodded. "I know." She picked up her glass. "I think I'll go in now. You can sit out here and finish your wine." She slipped into the cottage.

Aspen sagged down into her chair. She'd made a mess of everything now, hadn't she?

CHAPTER 13

Aspen got up first thing the next morning, made coffee, and headed over to Willow's cottage with a mug for her sister. Willow opened the door, fully dressed, her hair curled, and makeup on. Aspen ignored her own frayed shorts and t-shirt.

"Willow, I'm really sorry about last night. I shouldn't have said those things to you."

"It's okay. I know it was hard for you to hear how wonderful Denise thought Magnolia was." Willow took the offered mug. "I know you were really upset. And... you're right. I did have a wonderful childhood while yours was terrible. But look at your life now. It's as close to perfect as a person can get, don't you think? A wonderful man is marrying you. His family adores you. You have lots of friends here in Moonbeam."

"I know. I am lucky now. It was just hard to hear Denise go on and on about how wonderful Magnolia was."

"Sounds like she's against her brother and sister wanting to break the will."

"I still don't want Magnolia's money."

"Are you certain? You could do a lot with it. You and Walker could buy a nice home for the two of you. You wouldn't have to worry about money."

Aspen laughed. "I'm not sure I know how to live without worrying about money."

"Well, you could do something good with it. Use it for causes you believe in."

Aspen frowned. "I never thought of that."

"But we'll have to see how all of this shakes out with the legal troubles."

"Enough of talking about Magnolia. I want you to know how much I appreciate all you did to help me plan the wedding. I can't believe how much we got accomplished."

"It's all in the list-making." Willow grinned.

"You might make me a believer in lists after all."

Willow set her mug down. "I really should

get on the road. I want to get an early start. And I miss Eli terribly. I've video-chatted with him, but I've missed him so much."

"I'm sure you have."

"But it was a nice break. And I'll be back soon, I promise."

Aspen hugged her sister. "Thank you so much for coming. I'll miss you."

"I'll miss you, too." Willow grabbed her suitcase, and they walked out of the cottage.

"Text me when you get home to let me know you got home safely."

"I will." Willow gave her another quick hug, placed her suitcase in the back seat, and climbed into her car.

Aspen stood there watching her sister drive away. It had been quite a week. She was going to be glad to get back to her routine. Working here at the cottages and at Jimmy's. Seeing Walker more. And, with any luck, no wedding planning for a while.

She headed over to the office just as Rose and Violet were walking outside with their coffee. "Aspen, join us. Go grab some more coffee."

Aspen filled her mug and plunked down on

a chair beside Rose and Violet. "Willow just left."

"Did you have a nice visit with her?" Rose asked.

"I did. But I'm about all wedding planned out. I appreciate the help. I do. Who knew how many decisions had to be made and details figured out for a wedding?"

"My Emmett and I got married here. But there wasn't much to plan. I found a simple dress. Emmett bought me a bouquet of flowers. That was about it."

Aspen sighed. "That sounds so... wonderful."

Violet laughed. "I'm sure yours will be wonderful, too."

"Oh, it will. I'm sure." Because Willow hadn't left anything to chance. Every little detail had been figured out. Aspen shrugged. "I just want to be married to Walker. And I do want the day to be special. I just didn't know all that was involved."

"Is there much left to do or plan?" Rose asked.

"Nope. I swear we have everything planned out. Willow even made a schedule for the wedding day."

"She's quite the planner, huh?" Violet leaned back, smiling.

"She is. And I'm grateful. I just... need a break. But it was so wonderful to see her again. I still can't believe I have a sister. There's this... bond between us. I don't know how it survived all those years apart, but I can still feel it."

Rose set her cup down with a clatter.

Aspen looked at her closely. "Are you okay?"

"I... am." She sat back in her chair and sighed. "No, I don't think I am."

"Which is it?" Violet cocked her head to the side.

"I... I just have some decisions to make. I'm okay. Or I will be when I finally get things figured out."

"Better you than me. I'm all decided out." Aspen grinned.

Rose smiled. "I'm sure I'll feel better when I make my decision, too. One way or the other."

Rose enjoyed getting to know Em as the days passed. They took long beach walks and ate out at Jimmy's on the Wharf. They sat outside with George and watched the sunrise. Em joined her for coffee with Violet after Rose had a chance to explain to Violet a little bit about how Em had just suddenly appeared in her life.

Tonight they sat out on Rose's porch enjoying the evening, sipping sweet tea, and waiting to see what the sunset had in store for them. But the unspoken question still hung between them...

Em's phone rang, and she glanced at it. "It's Mom. I should get it."

Rose nodded.

"Hi, Mom. Yes, I'll be coming home soon. What?" Em glanced over at Rose. "How do you know that?"

"Yes, that's where I am. Moonbeam."

Rose looked up in surprise.

"Ah, the FindMe app. Yes, I decided to have a few days at the beach before coming home."

Rose looked over at Em, wishing she could hear the other side of the conversation.

"Why did I pick Moonbeam? Uh, it just sounded like a nice place to visit." Em listened for a moment. "No, Mom. I—" Em turned to Rose and covered the mic on her phone. "She... she wants to know if I'm here with you. She told me Moonbeam was your and Emmett's favorite place. I don't know what to tell her."

"You can tell her the truth." Rose's heart somersaulted. "You can tell her you're here visiting me and we're getting to know each other."

"Mom. Yes, I'm here with Rose. I'm sorry I didn't tell you. It's a long story. I'll explain when I get home." Em looked over at her again. "I... I don't know. I'll ask."

Em covered the mic again. "Mom wants to know if... if she could come here."

Rose wasn't sure she was ready for that, but Em's face held such a hopeful expression. She couldn't dash her hopes. "Okay. Yes. I think that will be okay." But would it?

"Rose said yes." Em glanced over at Rose again. "Okay, I'll pick you up at the Sarasota airport. Send me your flight info. I'll see you tomorrow."

Em put down her phone. "Well, that was... unexpected. My mom isn't very techie. But she keeps misplacing her purse, so I put one of those tags in it so she can track it with her phone. She lost her purse—again—and was looking at the app and, well, it's the same app that shows her where I am. And she saw I was here. I'm sorry. I didn't even think of that. That she could track me like that."

"That's okay. I think it was inevitable. And maybe it's time Pauline and I saw each other again. I'm just not sure…" She tried to gather her thoughts. This was so unexpected. She thought she'd have time to plan seeing Pauline again. On her timeline. Not just unexpectedly—tomorrow. "I'm not sure how it will all work out. I can't make you any promises."

"At least you're going to try. That's all I ask of you." Em stood. "I should probably go. Thanks for the tea. And I'll call you tomorrow when Mom gets to town."

Rose nodded. "Okay, I'll see you tomorrow."

Em left and Rose sat out on the deck, watching the sky turn golden shades of orange and yellow. A spectacular display. Her blue heron stalked along the water's edge.

Had she made the right decision? Was she ready to see Pauline? But now that she knew about Em and where she and Pauline lived, she couldn't just ignore the whole situation.

"Hey, you." George appeared at the bottom of the stairs. "Gorgeous sunset, isn't it?"

"It is. Come join me."

George settled into the chair next to her. "Where's Em tonight?"

"She was here. Just left. I think she wanted to give me some time." Rose turned to George. "I think she thought if she stayed, I'd change my mind."

"About what?"

"About meeting with my sister tomorrow."

George's eyebrows spiked. "You're actually meeting up with her?"

"I am. I'm just not sure how I feel about it."

"Well, one way or another, you've found her. And now you'll see her again. The rest of it? It will work out one way or the other. The way it's supposed to work out."

"I guess it will." She glanced up as the stars began to poke through the night sky. Yes, one way or the other, it was time to face the past. See what could be done with the huge rift between her and Pauline. And maybe things would work out, and maybe they wouldn't. But at least she could say she tried.

CHAPTER 14

R ose tidied her cottage the next morning. Unpacking a few more boxes and putting things away. She hung the painting that she and Emmett had bought over the entry table by the door. She placed a lantern filled with fairy lights at one end of the table and a cut-glass bowl filled with shells she'd been collecting on the other end.

Her heart raced every time she thought about seeing Pauline again, so she did her best to stay busy. Very busy. Who knew her good silver tray needed polishing right now and the door to the deck needed a thorough cleaning, inside and out? She considered cleaning the oven but didn't want to deal with the smell of the cleaner.

The floors could use a good mopping, so she did that next. Soon the tile floors sparkled.

Finally, tired, she made herself a cup of tea and sat at the kitchen table, willing herself to stay calm. It didn't really work, because every time she thought of seeing Pauline—and the last time she'd seen her—her heart began pounding.

That last time she'd seen Pauline…

Pauline had been buck naked and standing in her and Emmett's front room. And Emmett had been standing there with a shocked expression on his face.

She closed her eyes, willing the scene away. Not that it worked. That image was seared into her brain no matter how many millions of times she tried to erase it. Pauline. Without a stitch of clothes on.

"Hi, Mom." Em nervously greeted her mother at the airport. She'd gone inside to meet her where the passengers came out into the terminal.

Her mom gave her a hug. "Oh, Em. I missed you."

"Missed you, too. Did you check any luggage?"

"No, I just have my carry-on."

"Here, I'll take it." She took the handle. "Come on. I parked this way." If she kept up the small talk, she didn't have to think about why her mother was really here. And what was going to happen.

They got out to her car and her mother climbed in. Em put the suitcase in the back seat, then took a deep breath before getting into the car. She pulled out of the lot and headed out to University Parkway. The road was busy with the winter traffic as she threaded her way toward the highway that would take them to Moonbeam. She concentrated more than she probably needed to on the driving, but it kept her mind occupied.

Finally, she glanced over at her mom who was staring out the window. "Did you have a nice flight?" Meaningless chitchat was about all she could come up with.

"It was short." Her mother turned toward her. "A bit of a rough landing. I saw the pilot when we were deplaning. He didn't look like he was old enough to have a pilot's license, much less fly a big aircraft like that."

"I'm sure he's well-trained and old enough."

Silence dropped over them, stifling the moment. She tried again. "So, the weather looks like it will be nice for a few days."

"That's nice."

Stillness again.

She racked her brain for more to talk about, avoiding the thing she actually wanted to discuss. Rose. "Did you ever get a chance to join that book club you were thinking about joining? The one that meets at the library?"

"No, I was going to… but just haven't done it yet."

"You should. Then you could meet some new friends."

Her mom just nodded.

More silence. Then her mother broke the smothering quiet. "So how does Rose look?"

"She looks… good. I think Moonbeam agrees with her."

"What is she doing here? Staying at that old resort she loves so much?"

"Ah, no. She's moved here. Just a little bit ago. She had been staying at Blue Heron Cottages—she said it used to be Murphy's Place back when she and Emmett stayed there. She's made lots of friends here in town. She said she just needed a change. A chance to move on. She sold the house she lived in with Emmett."

"She did? That surprises me. I wouldn't think she'd want to move from a house that held so many memories for her."

"Maybe it had too many?"

Her mom stared at her for a moment. "I'm surprised she said she was okay with me coming here. I didn't think she ever wanted to see me again."

"Are you ever going to tell me what happened between you two?"

"I... I don't ever really talk about it. I don't like to even think about it. I made a mistake. A big one. The kind that people don't forgive you for."

"It's been a long time, though. Surely you two can work things out now?"

"That will really be up to Rose, I guess. Although I have to admit, even though I made such a bad mistake, I tried to tell her how sorry I was. To try and make it up to her. But she never would listen to me. She sent my letters back unopened. She hung up on me when I tried calling. It... hurt." Her mom looked out the window, quiet for a few moments. "But then, I hurt her, too."

"Well, I hope you two can see if you can find a way to work things out."

"I would like that, too."

CHAPTER 15

The doorbell rang. Rose slid her hands down her hips, a meager attempt at drying her sweaty palms. Her heart ricocheted in her chest. "You're fine, woman. Calm down," she said out loud. Not that it helped.

She took a quick look in the mirror and paused. What would Pauline think about her now? It had been so many years. They were both older now. Much older. She tucked a lock of her gray hair behind her ear.

With a long, deep breath, she headed for the door. Okay, here it was. The moment she'd been dreading for all these years.

She tugged the door open.

And there Pauline stood. Transformed by time, but still beautiful. Her hair was brown now, but Rose was sure the color came from a box. It wasn't exactly her sister's real chestnut brown hair color. She had wrinkles at the corners of her eyes. But her eyes were still that same warm blue color, a perfect mirror of her own. Her heart raced, and for an instant, she was swept back in time. To when they were inseparable. To when they shared their clothes, gossiped about kids in high school, and spent hours in their room talking and dreaming.

"Rose."

The single word pulled her out of the past.

Rose swallowed. "Pauline. Ah…" What to say? *Good to see you? Glad you're here? I'm still so mad at you?*

"I think I'll just give you two time to talk." Em swung her gaze between them, looking a bit leery. "I'm going to go take a walk on the beach."

Pauline nodded, never taking her eyes off Rose. Rose shifted under her gaze. What was her sister thinking? She used to swear she could read Pauline's thoughts. But not today. Not now.

Rose cleared her throat. "Ah… come in."

Her sister stepped into the cottage as Em walked away. Rose closed the door behind Pauline. "I made some sweet tea. Just a hint of

sugar, just like you like it. Would you like some?"
Is that how Pauline still liked her tea?

Pauline nodded and followed her into the kitchen. Rose got out two glasses, filled them with ice, and poured the tea. She handed one to Pauline, and the ice rattled as her sister took it.

They both stood staring at each other, holding their tea.

"We should go sit." Rose turned and headed to the main room. She sat in one of the chairs and Pauline settled on the edge of the couch, her back straight.

Pauline set her glass on a coaster on the coffee table, then looked up at her. "Em says you've moved here permanently."

"I have. I bought this cottage. I love it. And did you see the color of it?"

Pauline flashed a small smile. "I did. Your perfect shade of teal."

So Pauline remembered things too. "It is. Isn't that strange? And the cottage seemed to call to me to live here. Like I belonged or something. Like I'd been here before. I know that sounds strange."

Pauline gave her a tentative smile. "Maybe it feels that way because... I've stayed here before."

"Here? In my cottage?"

"Yes. It was a rental. I was feeling so lonely one year. Em was away at college. I knew that you and Emmett came here for your anniversary each year. So I... I rented this cottage. I just wanted... a glimpse of you. To make sure you were okay."

"You were watching us?"

"No, not really. I did see you two out shelling on the beach a few times. But I stayed inside. I didn't want you to know I was here." The corners of Paulines lips curved into a smile. "But the teal color? That was my doing. The owner came by with his painter while I was here. They had some paint samples. They were having a hard time picking out the color to paint the cottage. I steered them to this color."

"I... I don't even know what to say." Was that why this house felt so familiar to her? Was she picking up on her sister being here? Was that connection still there after all these years?

"I'm glad you said I could come here. I thought... I thought maybe I'd never see you again. That you'd never want to see me."

Rose stared at her sister, seeing both the pain and the hope in her eyes. But she wasn't sure she could give her what she wanted. "Pauline, I'm still hurt. When I think of what I walked in on…"

"Nothing happened."

"I know that. I trust Emmett. But you stood there with your dress pooled down at your feet as naked as the day you were born. Standing in front of my husband. I—to this day—can't figure out why. You're my sister. How could you do that? Why?"

Pauline sat silent for a few moments. "I know it was wrong. And I tried to explain to you why… but you wouldn't listen. Not that my why makes it right."

"Why don't you explain your why to me now?" Her hand shook, so she set her glass down on the table beside her and then looked up to watch Pauline's face closely.

"I had just found out… I found out I was pregnant. I panicked. I'd slept with this guy. A one-night thing. He was just traveling through town. You know, to this day, I don't even know his last name."

"That doesn't sound like something you'd do."

"I'd had a big fight with Daddy. And I felt like you deserted me when you married

Emmett. Left me to deal with Daddy on my own."

She hadn't really thought about how her getting married had left Pauline to deal with their father on her own. "But I still don't understand how this all ties into you being naked in my front room."

"After I found out I was pregnant, I came up with this wild idea... Emmett was such an honorable guy. I thought if I could convince him to sleep with me, I could then say the baby was his. Then I knew he'd help me raise it."

Rose sat back in her chair, astonished. "And that was your plan? And you didn't care who got hurt? Whose life you'd ruin? You didn't think about... me?"

"I hadn't thought it out that far. I was just desperate for... a solution. So you were gone that night, and I went over and made Emmett a couple of stiff drinks."

"Emmett didn't drink much."

"No, he didn't. But I thought maybe if I got him loosened up... and then I... well, I slipped off my dress. I thought he'd want me."

"I can't believe that you'd even think of doing that. I'm your sister. Emmett was my husband."

"Well, you didn't have to worry. He didn't want me. He had just told me to put on my clothes and leave when you walked in the door."

"I never doubted Emmett for a moment. He wouldn't cheat on me."

"No, he wouldn't. And I should have known that. It was a stupid, crazy plan. And I was so ashamed of what I did. Of what I planned to do. That I'd even think it was okay to try to seduce Emmett. I was so young and foolish. And so very afraid. And very alone." Tears rolled down Pauline's face. "But that's no excuse. I'm so, so sorry. It was a really terrible thing to do."

"And yet, Emmett found a way to forgive you, didn't he?" Rose said softly.

"He did. And he helped Em and me when we most needed it. I don't know why he helped us. He shouldn't have after what I did. But he said he had to help Em. That she wasn't a part of... of what I did." Pauline swiped at her tears. "And I don't expect you to ever forgive me. I'm just thankful to have the chance to tell you how very sorry I am."

Rose sat there, staring at her sister. And then, miraculously, all the anger she'd been hanging onto for all these years began to slip away. Not totally gone, but pushed back a manageable distance.

She wasn't ready to say she forgave Pauline, but she wasn't ready to push her sister out of her life again, either.

Rose stared at her sister in silence for a few moments. "I'm really... happy to have you here. To see you again. I've... missed you."

Pauline jumped up. "You have? I've missed you so much. Desperately. We were so close, and I ruined everything."

"I'm sorry Daddy kicked you out. Emmett told me that in his letter. It must have been scary to face having a child all alone."

"He did throw me out. I've never seen him so angry. Madder than when he found out that you married Emmett. He said I disgraced the family name. And he never wanted to see me again. And I just didn't know what to do..."

"You know, Daddy called me to come see him as he was dying. And he never said one word about you having a child. And I couldn't understand why you didn't come to his funeral. I thought maybe you didn't because I was there."

"Oh, I was there. I just... hung back. So you wouldn't see me. But I had to say my goodbyes to him. Even if he didn't want to say them to me."

Rose could see the raw pain in her sister's eyes. About being disowned by their father. And the regret about what had happened with Emmett. That was clearly etched in her features.

"I... I didn't know all this back then. That you were pregnant. Or that Daddy kicked you out. I thought you just had enough of him and left." Rose sighed. "I wish things had been different. That I'd know you were pregnant. I would have helped you with Em. I would have."

"You wouldn't take my calls. And you returned my letters unopened. I finally decided I should leave town before people could tell I was pregnant. I figured I had to find a way to do it alone."

Rose took Pauline's hand. "I'm so sorry you had to do all that alone. Raise Em alone. It must have been so hard."

Pauline stared down at their hands before looking directly at her. "It was at times. But I wouldn't trade a thing. A silly mistake—a one-night stand—when I was young led to the biggest blessing in my life." She shook her head. "If only I hadn't made such a terrible mistake with Emmett... things might have been so different."

"And if I would have listened to you all those years ago, maybe I would have understood what you did in desperation. Not that it was right. And you hurt me so badly. Betrayed me."

"I know I did. I'm so sorry."

Rose stood silently, her gaze taking in every inch of her sister. The woman she'd once been so close to that it was like they were one. And she'd never given her sister a moment to explain. She shoved Pauline away just like their father had. Pauline had been deserted by her whole family right when she needed them most.

Guilt seeped through her at the part she'd unknowingly played in all of this too. Why had she just not talked to her sister? Read even one of her letters?

Rose swallowed. "You know what? I would like for us... for us to get past all this. To forget about what happened back then. You've raised a wonderful woman, and I'm so grateful to have had the chance to get to know her this week. And I'm sorry I didn't just listen to you back then. I was to wrapped up in how *I* felt. Do you think... that we could find a way to... be a family again?"

The tears poured down her sister's cheeks. "I'd like nothing more in the whole world."

And just like that, Rose's heart started to thaw, and she took a step forward, pulling her sister into her arms. And it felt so very, very right.

Her tears mingled with Pauline's as they clung to each other.

CHAPTER 16

Em walked along the shoreline letting the waves lap at her feet. She walked a long way before turning around, giving Rose and her mom as much time as they needed. She just hoped when she returned that her mother wasn't sitting outside in the car, all alone, waiting for her.

If only the two of them could find a way to make peace with the past. She wanted that. For them. For herself. But her mom said she'd made a terrible mistake and wouldn't blame Rose if she never forgave her. But maybe enough years had gone by?

She paused at the water's edge in front of Rose's cottage. Had she given them enough time? Maybe she should walk some more.

George came out of his cottage and waved to her as he jogged down to the shoreline. "Hello, Em. Taking a walk?"

"I was. Now I'm trying to decide if I should go inside or not. Mom and Rose are in there. At least I hope Mom is still in there."

"Ah, Rose told me your mom was coming today. She wasn't sure how it would go. If the past could be put in the past."

"Did she tell you what happened between them?"

"No. And I didn't ask. I know it was enough to thrust them apart for all these years."

"I just hope they can work it out. That we can be a family now." She stared up at the cottage, longing to know what was going on in there, but dreading it too. What if they couldn't work it out? If all her hoping was for nothing?

"Look. There they are." George pointed to the cottage where Rose and her mom were stepping outside.

She squared her shoulders. "Well, at least Mom is still here."

Rose waved, motioning for her to come up to the cottage.

"Looks like she wants you to come join

them. Good luck. I hope things work out for you. For all of you."

"Thanks, George." She headed across the sand, each step taking her closer. Soon she'd know if they'd worked things out. She slowly climbed the stairs, delaying hearing the answer she was craving... or finding out it hadn't worked out like she wanted.

"Em, come join us. I brought out some sweet tea. I have a glass for you if you want some." Rose motioned to a tray with a pitcher of tea and three glasses. That was a good sign, right?

"I'd love some." She looked at Rose, then her mother. What had happened? At least her mom was still here. A tiny ray of hope began to creep through her. She tried to tamp it back, but it refused. It clung to her, shining its beam to the future she wanted.

Her mother walked over to her and wrapped her arm around her waist. "You should know. Rose and I have worked things out. She's forgiven me."

Tears sprang to the corners of her eyes. "Oh, Mom. That's good news." And just like that, the tiny ray sprang into a brilliant blaze of happiness and hope.

"And we agreed we're just not going to talk again about what happened between us. It's in the past," Rose said as she handed a glass of tea to her, then to her mom.

"Yes, the past is the past. But now... now we want to try to figure out our future," her mother said.

"Make up for lost time. I'm so sorry I didn't get to know you when you were young. Watch you grow up. I'm sorry I wasn't there to help Pauline. And I'm... I'm glad Emmett could help some, even if he kept it a secret from me."

"That was my fault. I made him promise when he first found out and contacted me. I was hurt that both you and our father had cut me out of your lives. But over the years, I should have softened. I should have let him tell you." Her mother's eyes clouded with sadness. "I've made so many mistakes."

"Maybe this was just how it was all supposed to work out. I don't know. I'm just glad that Emmett sent me that letter. That we got to see each other again and make amends. That I gave you a chance to explain. But, the past is the past, right? Now we still have the future." Rose lifted her glass. "To a bright future as a family and figuring out what it will be like for the three of us."

"To family." Em raised her glass, no longer trying to hold back her tears. She'd gotten her wish. She had her family back together. The one she never thought she'd have.

CHAPTER 17

Violet sat on the porch with Rose a few months later, having their coffee. Violet had a pad of paper and was busy scribbling notes. "So, I called Willow, and she can come to Moonbeam on the weekend we picked for Aspen's bridal shower. She was so excited and wanted to know what she could do to help. I told her we had everything under control, but she could help us set up the day of the shower." She frowned as she looked at the list, hoping she wasn't forgetting anything she needed to do.

"I can't wait. I think it will be lovely."

"Evelyn is going to make the food, thank goodness. That's not really my thing." Violet laughed. "And you said you'd get flowers from

Daisy and do the floral arrangements. It sure helps that you used to work at a flower shop."

"George said he'd help Danny put up the tent canopy in the courtyard. That way, it won't be quite so warm. And if it rains, we'll still be okay."

"Aspen made me swear we wouldn't do any games. So I'm not sure what we'll do the whole time."

"Aspen will open the gifts, of course. We'll keep a list of who gives her what. And people can just chat. I'm sure there'll be lots of wedding talk going on." Rose reached for the pad and pen. "Let me make some notes. We'll need to set up the chairs that morning. Oh, and how about we make a nice fruit punch?"

"That sounds good."

"I could make ice cubes with pieces of fruit in them. That would look festive. I saw some in a magazine I was reading. I'll get everything for the punch and do the ice cubes. They froze the cubes in silicone cupcake trays."

"That sounds fun."

"I want it to be nice for Aspen. I'm so happy for her." Rose set down the paper and pen.

"It's just next month that she gets married. This winter just flew by, didn't it? I think it will be a lovely wedding. And Willow has it all planned down to the last detail, according to Aspen."

"Aspen said she really appreciated Willow's help." Rose picked up her cup and took a sip.

"So, have you talked to your sister recently?" Violet looked over the rim of her cup.

"I have. I video-chatted with Pauline and Em just the other day. Em got me all set up with a tablet and showed me how to do it. We talk every week. They're going to come visit soon."

"I'm so glad that it all worked out for you." Violet still didn't know what had caused the split with the sisters but didn't ask. She was just grateful that Rose had family now, especially after losing Emmett. The sad, haunted look in her eyes was gone now, and she looked so relaxed. She laughed a lot now and had made more friends here in Moonbeam. She'd joined a knitting group that met at the Methodist church each Wednesday and a book club that Collette was running once a month at her Beachside Bookshop. And Rose and George went out to dinner about once a week, but Violet was sure they were just friends.

"So, how are Danny and Allison doing? All settled into their new house?" Rose asked.

"They are. And Allison is doing well in school here and loves her job at Sea Glass Cafe."

"Looks like you and Danny are getting kind of serious, aren't you?" Rose raised her eyebrows.

"I guess so. It's not like either one of us is dating other people."

"And he makes you happy. That's what's important."

"He does. I wasn't looking for a relationship, but it just... happened. I can't imagine my life without Danny in it. And now that he's moved to Moonbeam, Robbie has stopped with all the helpful advice about being careful and how Danny was going to hurt me."

Rose laughed. "He was just being the protective older brother."

"Yeah, he has a lot of opinions about a lot of things." She grinned. "Good thing I still adore him. He is a great brother to have." She stood. "I guess I should get back to work. I have accounting stuff to do." She made a face. "Not my favorite task."

"I should go, too. I'm grocery shopping this morning. Having George over for dinner." Rose stood. "Thanks for the coffee. I'll see you soon."

Rose headed across the courtyard, and Violet picked up their empty cups. Yes, she was sure Rose and George were just friends. Pretty sure... And it didn't hurt Rose to have a special friend now, did it?

CHAPTER 18

Aspen threw her arms around Willow. "You're here."

"Of course, I'm here." Willow hugged her back. "I couldn't miss your shower, could I?"

"I still can't believe all this is happening. A bridal shower. The wedding. I feel like I'm living in some fairy tale."

"You deserve it." Willow tugged Aspen's hand. "Now, come sit down out here on the porch with me. Tell me everything that's happened since I left."

"Not much, really. I did have my final fitting for the wedding dress. It really is beautiful. I appreciate you letting me borrow it."

"It means a lot to me that you'll get married in the same dress I did. There were so many years that we didn't get to share anything as sisters. And now we can." Willow smiled and stretched out her legs. "I've sure missed being here. I mean, I love being back home with Eli and Derek, but there's just something so peaceful and relaxing about Moonbeam. Especially here at the cottages."

"I love it here. I can't believe that Magnolia finally did something right by me. By sending me here to Moonbeam."

"Oh, that reminds me. A couple of things. The lawyer called, and he's pretty sure the judge is going to side with Mr. Wilkerson's kids. If we only had the divorce papers, maybe that would help. His kids' lawyer has convinced the judge that Magnolia tricked Mr. Wilkerson." Willow shrugged. "So I don't know."

"Well, it is what it is. We can't change the outcome. The legal system will just have to work it out."

"We can always appeal the decision." Willow looked over at her.

"And let it drag on for years? No thanks. Whatever will be, will be." Aspen shook her head. "What's the other thing you wanted to say?"

"The detective Derek hired has another new lead on finding Dad."

"Doesn't he always?" Aspen refused to get her hopes up.

"He feels like this one is a good one. And I hope he's right."

"I guess we'll see how that turns out, too, won't we?"

"Oh, and you have to let me do something." Willow tilted her head to the side. "Please don't say no."

"What is it?" She eyed her sister.

"Let me take you shopping this afternoon. Let's find you a fun outfit for the shower."

"You don't have to do that." Though she had to admit she'd been wondering what in her closet was appropriate to wear. She hadn't wanted to spend money on a new dress with all they were spending on the wedding.

"I want to. Please let me. I'm just excited to have a sister to shop with." Willow grinned. "So you can't disappoint me."

Aspen laughed. "Oh, I see. You think this is all about you."

Willow joined in her laughter. "Yes, all about me. So, yes? We'll go shopping?"

"Yes, we'll go shopping. We can go to

Barbara's Boutique. I'm sure we can find something there."

"Perfect." She jumped up. "Let's go."

"Oh, you mean right now?" Aspen rose. "Okay, then let's get this shopping trip going."

They went to Barbara's and Aspen swore Willow had her try on two dozen dresses. This one was too long. That one the wrong color. The next one too loose. Finally, they found one they both agreed was perfect. And it made Aspen feel slightly less guilty when she saw it was on sale. Willow bought the dress, and they headed outside.

"So, what next?" Willow asked.

Aspen's lips twitched into a smile. "What? You don't have the rest of our day all planned out?"

She laughed. "Nope, nothing until I'm going to help Violet and Rose set up for the shower tomorrow. We are free women. What would you like to do?"

"Honestly? Pick up some sandwiches for dinner. Go back to the cottages and kick back and relax. I feel like I'm running so hard these days."

"Then that's what we'll do. I brought a nice bottle of wine and it's chilling in the fridge.

We'll eat and then sit out on the porch and sip wine and watch the sunset."

"Can't think of a better way to spend an evening." She hugged Willow. "I'm so glad you're here."

Willow tucked her arm in Aspen's and they headed back to the car, ready for their relaxing girls' night in.

CHAPTER 19

Aspen couldn't believe how many people were at the bridal shower. She was ridiculously happy that Willow had made her get a new dress. It really was perfect for the occasion.

The courtyard had been converted into a magical paradise of flowers, ribbons, and decorations that perfectly matched her wedding colors.

Walker's mother, Mrs. Bodine, hurried over to her. "Oh, Aspen. You look lovely. And look what Violet did out here. What a truly wonderful transformation." She gave Aspen a quick hug. "Tara will be along soon. She got tied up at work but promised she wouldn't be more than twenty minutes behind me. She's quite excited about being Walker's best man. Or whatever you'd call it when a woman is the best man."

"I'm glad she's in the wedding, too."

"I can't believe it's coming up so soon. Seems like it was just Christmas and Walker was proposing to you."

"It did go by quickly, didn't it?"

"And I'm so happy to have you joining our family. You make my son so happy, and that makes me happy." Mrs. Bodine reached out and squeezed her hand.

Aspen tried hard to fight back the tears that threatened to spill. "Thank you. You all have been so accepting of me. Made me feel so welcome."

"Well, you're family now. Hope you can handle our huge clan."

There were a ton of Bodines. Aunts, uncles, cousins. She was just barely getting all their names straight.

Tara came hurrying up to them. "Told you I wouldn't be far behind you, Mom. Oh, Aspen, you look great."

"Willow took me shopping for this dress."

"Well, I really like it. I should have thought to look for something new to wear, too."

Tara looked lovely in a floral print dress that hugged her slim silhouette. She had on cute red flats that matched the flower pattern. Aspen was amazed that someone would just have the perfect dress hanging in her closet like that. She wondered if she'd ever have that kind of closet. Maybe if Willow got her way and kept taking her shopping.

"Anyway, it's nice to be out of the Jimmy's on the Wharf shirts and into real clothes."

Violet walked up to them. "I think it's time to open the presents."

Aspen followed Violet over to the table laden with packages all wrapped so prettily. It would be a shame to unwrap them. They all looked so lovely.

Willow motioned for her to take a seat. "I took some pictures of the gift table. It looks so great, doesn't it? And I took some pics of the food table, too. And all the decorations. I'm going to get them printed and make you an album so you can remember all the details of the shower."

"Thank you." Her sister honestly thought of everything.

They went to sit by the table and she carefully unwrapped each gift while Willow wrote down what the gift was and who gave it to her. She was going to have a million thank-you notes to write. Luckily, Willow had also thought to buy a big box of thank-you cards in the same blue color that she was using in the wedding.

Occasionally, she wasn't sure what something was, but her sister would quickly make a comment about the item to clue her in. Who knew there were so many strange cooking implements she knew nothing about? She unwrapped a package with a lacy negligee in it and sheepishly glanced over at her future mother-in-law.

"Oh, that's pretty." Willow snatched it from the box and held it up. "Should come in handy on your honeymoon," she teased.

The heat of a blush burned Aspen's face as she reached for the next box. After opening what seemed like a million gifts, she finally reached the last one.

"That's from me,'" Mrs. Bodine said.

Aspen carefully unwrapped the lovely white paper and precisely tied bow. She gasped when she opened the box. "Oh, these are so beautiful." She held them up. "Look, they have our initials and our wedding date."

"Those are engraved toasting glasses to use for the toasts at the wedding. I thought they'd make a nice keepsake of the wedding for you."

She got up and hugged Mrs. Bodine. "Thank you so much. What a thoughtful gift."

People began to stand up and mill around. Violet had put out so much food. Trays of petit fours, a fruit tray, and mini cucumber sandwiches cut into squares. And a big bowl of punch with cute fruit ice cubes floating in it. It all looked so elegant. Like nothing she'd ever been to. Was this the kind of thing most women went to regularly?

Willow wrapped an arm around her waist. "It's all really lovely, isn't it?"

"It is. Kind of overwhelming. I can't believe how many people showed up."

"Look at all these friends you've made here in Moonbeam."

"I guess I really have. Though, I'm sure a lot of them came because I'm marrying into the Bodine family. Everyone knows and loves the Bodines."

Willow hugged her. "And they love you, too.

And so do I. I'm so happy you're back in my life."

And in that one moment, Aspen was certain her life was perfect. She had friends, a new family, a newfound sister… and Walker.

CHAPTER 20

The next morning Aspen could hardly move around her cottage. It was piled high with gifts from the shower. She'd have to figure out where to put them so she could at least get around.

And then... she and Walker still needed to find a place to live. Neither his apartment nor her cottage was big enough for them to really live in. Walker said he didn't care where they lived, as long as he was with her. But she was sure he wouldn't be happy in her tiny two-bedroom, one-bath cottage.

She glanced at the clock and hurried out to meet Willow. Her sister greeted her with a piping hot mug of coffee. "Thought you might want this. We sure stayed up late last night talking."

"We did. But it was fun, wasn't it? I love hearing about your life and getting to know you better." Aspen sank onto a chair on the porch.

"I don't usually stay up that late, though. Always up early with Eli."

"I don't stay up late either. But I can make an exception when my sister comes to town." She glanced over at Willow and grinned. "So, I guess you have our whole day planned for today, don't you?"

Willow shook her head slightly. "No, actually. I thought we'd wing it today. We could swim in the ocean. Or go for a nice beach walk. Or go out to eat somewhere. Whatever the bride wants."

"Really? I thought you were the ultimate planner of all things."

"I am. But I'm taking a break." Willow's eyes twinkled as she took a sip of her coffee.

They both turned at the sound of someone approaching the cottage. Willow jumped up. "Derek. What are you doing here? Is everything all right?"

"Yes, everything is fine. I just... wanted to

bring Aspen a present for her shower. It's actually a present for both of you."

Aspen got up and stood by her sister. "Hi, Derek. You didn't need to get me anything."

"Ah, but I did." He turned around and motioned to someone. An older man came walking up to them.

Aspen stared at the man. He seemed... familiar.

"Aspen, Willow... this is... your father." A wide smile spread across Derek's face and he flung out his arm wide.

Willow gasped and clutched at Aspen's hand. The longer Aspen looked at him, the more she saw hints of memories in the features of his face. She took a step down off the porch and toward him. "Dad?"

The man nodded and opened his arms. She raced forward and crumbled into his embrace as he held her tightly. Then he opened one arm and reached out for Willow. She ran forward and into his arms. Aspen's tears mingled with Willow's and their father's.

They all finally stepped back. Their father swept his hand across his face, then looked from one to the other. "I can't believe it. My girls. I never thought I'd see you again."

"When I was just a little kid, Magnolia told me you left us," Aspen said. "But then the lawyer gave us this letter from her—after she died." Aspen caught herself. "You did know Magnolia was gone, right?"

"I did. Derek told me." Her father nodded.

"In her letter, she said you hadn't really left us. That she took me and *she* left you. I can't understand how she could do that. To you. To me." She tried to tamp down her anger toward Magnolia.

"I came back, and she was gone. All of you were gone. I tried everything I could think of to find you. All her favorite places. People she knew. But I couldn't find you. I was... heartbroken. I mean, your mother and I weren't a very good match, but I loved both of you so much. And then... you were both gone."

"Yes, Magnolia gave Willow up for adoption but kept me with her. Probably to cook for her and clean, or who knows why. She left me for weeks at a time. All alone."

Her father stepped forward and pulled her into his arms again. "I'm so, so sorry. I did try to find you. It wasn't as easy to find people back then. And I didn't have any luck tracking down

Magnolia after things did get easier with the Internet and everything."

She reveled in the feeling of being in her father's arms. His strong arms. And his strong hand stroked her back, soothing her. She finally stepped out of his embrace.

"Well, it appears Magnolia married four times... so that would get harder and harder. Though, the lawyer said he can't find a divorce for you two, so I'm not sure they were real, legal marriages."

"I never signed one."

Aspen sighed. "So, she didn't really legally marry all these men she said she was married to. So like Magnolia."

Her father turned to Willow. "And Willow, look at you. All grown up. You were just a wee one when Magnolia took you away. And she gave you up for adoption? I guess she forged my signature on that, too. I would never have agreed to it."

Derek walked over and slipped his arm around Willow's shoulder. "So, this time, the detective's lead panned out. He found Trent and as soon as Trent heard, he wanted to see you. I thought it best to bring him to Moonbeam since both of you were here."

Her father looked around at the cottages and frowned. "So it looks like Murphy really fixed up the place."

"You knew the cottages when they were Murphy's Place? He doesn't own it now. Violet bought the resort and fixed it all up."

"I did know it back then. It was your uncle Murphy's resort. We stayed here a time or two. It was one of the first places I came looking for you after Magnolia disappeared. But Murphy said he had no clue where his sister was."

"Murphy was our uncle? I don't remember that." Aspen frowned. "I think... I think Magnolia and I lived here for a while after you left. I mean... after she took us away."

"So Murphy lied to me? Hid the fact you were here?"

"Maybe. I guess?" It tore at Aspen's heart to see the sadness in her father's eyes.

"I missed so much of your lives. I want to get to know you two. All about you."

"Well, you've met my husband, Derek," Willow said. "And Aspen is getting married in a few weeks."

"Really?" Her father's eyes lit up.

"Yes. I am. To Walker. And..." She walked up to her father and took his hand. "I'd like nothing more than for you to walk me down the aisle. To give me away. I never thought that could happen. Will you?"

He brushed back a lock of her hair and looked straight into her eyes. "I'll never give you away, never lose you again. But I'd be honored to walk you down the aisle to your husband."

"Oh, Dad." And she threw herself into his arms again, crying. With sadness for all they'd missed and what Magnolia had done to all of them, and with happiness that they were finally all reunited. She held out her hand, and Willow grabbed it.

"Finally, I have my girls back," their father whispered.

"And we have our dad." They stood there with tears in their eyes, none of them wanting to break the spell of joy that surrounded them.

CHAPTER 21

Aspen could hardly believe her father was standing here. Standing right in front of her like all these years had just disappeared in an instant. Only... the loss of not having him around for all that time clung to them. They had lost so much time and had so much to make up for.

"Why don't we go somewhere where we can talk?" her dad said. "I have so many questions. So much I want to know."

Willow nodded. "Yes, let's do that."

"I'm afraid I'm going to have to bow out," Derek said. "I've got to get back to Eli. Mom's watching him now. But I couldn't miss seeing you two finally get to meet your dad."

Willow kissed Derek. "Thank you for

everything you did to help us. For finding the detective, for bringing Dad here."

"I'll see you back at home. Stay as long as you want. I've got everything covered."

"Thanks, hon. You're the best."

Derek waved and headed to his car. Aspen frowned, trying to think of the perfect place to suggest they go.

Willow jumped in. "How about Jimmy's on the Wharf? That's your favorite restaurant, right, Aspen?" Her eyes sparkled with amusement.

Aspen laughed. "Yes, Jimmy's sounds perfect. Then Dad will get to meet Walker."

She couldn't wait for Walker to meet her dad. How had she gone from all alone in the world to having a sister—and now a father—in just a few short months?

They all headed out toward the wharf. She walked on one side of their father and Willow on the other. Both of them had their arms tucked in his. A family of three. Her emotions were in overdrive, and she ping-ponged between chasing back tears and wanting to dance a jig right there on the sidewalk, not caring who saw her. She excitedly pointed out different places in Moonbeam as they walked along, wanting to share her town with her father. She pointed to the brick building across the street. "That's Parker's General Store and right next door is Sea Glass Cafe. That's a great place to eat, too. Even though I'm partial to Jimmy's, of course. Walker's family owns it, and I work there, too."

"Can't wait to meet your young man."

"And that's The Cabot Hotel." She pointed to the expansive hotel as they walked past.

"That sure looks different. As I remember it, it was looking a little rundown last time I saw it."

"Delbert Hamilton bought it and restored it. I think it's so beautiful now. So elegant. And you should see the ballroom. It's magical." Aspen laughed. "I have so much to show you. People I want you to meet. I guess I shouldn't try to cram it all into one day."

"The town sure has changed since the last time I was here looking for your mother. Of course, that was years ago. And I can't believe that you ended up living here, Aspen."

"Best thing that ever happened to me," she said, then laughed again. "And finding out about Willow and you coming back into our lives, those are right up there with the best thing ever, too."

"It sure is," Willow agreed as they

approached the entrance to the wharf. As they headed down the long wharf, Aspen pointed out the other restaurants, the candy shop, a candle store, and a gift shop that carried art from local artists. At the end of the wharf, Aspen led them into the restaurant.

Tara was at the reception desk. "Well, hello there. Didn't know you were coming in tonight."

"Tara, this is… my dad."

Tara's eyes widened. "Your dad? Wow. Nice to meet you, Mr. Caldwell."

"Trent, call me Trent."

"Let me get you a table, and I've got to find Walker. But I'll let you tell him the news. He'll be thrilled for you."

Soon after they were seated, Walker came hurrying across the restaurant, threading his way between the tables. "Aspen, I didn't know you were coming in. Tara said you had something to tell me."

"There's someone I want you to meet." She gave Walker a quick hug. "It was a last-minute thing because… Walker, this is my father."

"What?" Walker's eyes widened and his mouth spread into a wide grin. "You found him."

Her father reached out his hand. "Nice to

meet the man who's going to marry my daughter."

Walker pumped her father's hand. "So great to meet you, too, sir."

Just then Mrs. Bodine walked up. "Tara said I should come over and say hi."

"This is Mrs. Bodine. And Mrs. Bodine, this is my dad."

"Oh, Aspen. That's wonderful. You found him." Mrs. Bodine hugged Aspen's father. "Oh, hope that was okay. I'm a hugger. And I'm just so happy for Aspen and Willow. They've been trying so hard to find you."

"And I'm glad they did. This is the best day ever, meeting my girls again."

"Walker, you join them. I'll get someone to cover your work for a bit," Mrs. Bodine insisted.

"Thanks, Mom."

They all settled back into their chairs. Aspen looked around the table. Her sister. Her father. Walker. Her heart soared with happiness. Her family all having a meal together. Something she'd never have thought was possible before coming to Moonbeam.

Her father ordered champagne for the table. After it came, Willow raised her glass. "I think we should make a toast to Magnolia."

Aspen stared at her in disbelief. "What?"

"Because… she finally did the right thing by us before she died. Made sure Aspen and I found each other again. Told us that Dad didn't desert us, that she left him. Which eventually led to today."

Aspen still wasn't certain she could toast her mother. Not after all she'd done.

Her father raised his glass. "To Magnolia. She made some terrible mistakes. Ones that are hard to forgive or forget. But thank goodness she had a change of heart in the end. May she rest in peace."

Everyone looked at her as she sat, her wine glass still sitting on the table in front of her. A tiny chunk of the ice in her heart where she kept her feelings about Magnolia began to melt. She could hold a grudge forever. Be angry forever. And never forgive her mother.

She looked at Walker who seemed to read her every thought. He leaned closer and whispered, "It's up to you. Everyone understands and loves you."

She took a deep breath and reached for her glass, raising it up to the others. "To Magnolia. Who finally got something right. To Willow, my fabulous sister. And finding my dad." She turned to Walker. "And to Walker. The most wonderful husband-to-be in the world."

"To family," her father said.

And with the clinks of their glasses, Aspen did feel like she was right in the midst of family. Surrounded by love. Safe. Home. And a bit more of the bitterness toward Magnolia melted.

Magnolia had brought her to Moonbeam. And Moonbeam had brought her all of this.

CHAPTER 22

The last week had been an exhausting blur of last-minute wedding prep. Willow texted her with questions multiple times a day. Had she double-checked the RSVPs? Did Rose get the vases for the flowers? Had she picked up the ribbon they were tying into bows for the chairs on the aisle?

She finished up her last shift working the reception desk at the cottages and headed for her cottage, wanting nothing more than to put her feet up and veg in front of the TV.

She kicked off her shoes, sank onto the couch, and put her feet up. Just as she reached for the remote, there was a knock at the door. With a groan, she pushed off the couch and headed to answer it.

Walker stood there with a bouquet of flowers that he thrust at her. "Here. These are for you."

"I thought you were working tonight." She stood on her tiptoes and kissed him before taking the offered flowers. "These are lovely."

"I thought you needed a break tonight. From the planning and everything going on. A night of just the two of us."

"That sounds perfect." It did. But she didn't really feel like going out to eat with the crowds of people, and she didn't really have anything to make for supper for the two of them.

"Put the flowers in water and come with me. I have a surprise for you."

She eyed him. "What is it?"

"Well, that wouldn't be a surprise then, would it?"

He was dressed in nice shorts and a collared shirt. She looked at her Blue Heron Cottages t-shirt and worn shorts. "Where are we going? I need to change."

"You look fine."

"Give me a minute to freshen up." She hurried to her room and slipped on a simple dress, brushed her hair, and put on some lipstick. Within a few minutes, she was back out to the front room where Walker waited patiently.

"Let's go." He opened the door. "We're walking if that's okay."

She nodded. He led her down the sidewalk and down the streets, cutting across to the road that ran along the beach. They finally made it to the beach access and headed over the ramp, which was covered with a scatter of rose petals. She quickly looked up at him and he flashed a smile.

"You should probably follow them."

She slipped off her shoes and couldn't hold back her smile as she followed the path of the petals, with Walker walking beside her across the sand. She let out a little gasp as they went over the rise and saw what Walker had done. She paused to take in the incredible scene stretching out before her. A table with two chairs sat near the edge of the shoreline, cast in the glow of two lanterns. A big bouquet sat in the middle of the table. The timing was perfect, with just the beginning of the sunset flinging itself across the sky.

"Oh, Walker, this is wonderful." She threw herself into his arms. "No crowds. Just us. It's lovely."

They crossed over to the table, and she saw a line of candles in mason jars leading to the water's edge. "I thought we could have some champagne before our dinner."

He led her down the lighted pathway to a blanket spread on the sand. An ice bucket with a bottle of champagne sat waiting for them. Two champagne flutes rested beside it. She dropped down onto the blanket and tucked her legs beneath her. Walker poured them each a glass of champagne and handed one to her. "To us. To a night of just the two of us."

"Oh, I'll drink to that." She slowly relaxed as they sipped their drinks. She hadn't realized just how stressed and rushed she'd been the last few weeks. This was the perfect antidote.

"I don't know how you always know exactly what I need, exactly when I need it." She leaned against his shoulder. "And I sure don't know how you pulled all this off."

"I can't take all the credit. Tara helped me finish setting things up while I went to get you. She was in on the surprise. Do you like it?"

"Like it? I love it. It's all so wonderful."

Walker stood and held down a hand. "Let's eat." He helped her to her feet, then threaded his arm around her waist as they walked back to the table. He pulled out a chair for her and she sat down.

He turned around to a cooler and pulled out an insulated container. "Mom assured me the meal would stay hot in these. Let's see if she was right." He opened the containers and smiled. "She was right. Of course. Mom is always right."

He dished up grilled shrimp with sides of steamed green beans and roasted potatoes. Slices of fresh baked bread with slabs of butter completed the dinner. "This looks wonderful."

"And we have chocolate-covered strawberries for dessert. I wasn't quite sure how to make them, but Tara looked up some recipes on the internet and I think—I hope—they turned out okay."

Her heart swelled with love for this man. For all the effort he'd gone to in making this a special night for her. The sunset decided it was time to show off, and the sky erupted into a brilliance of splashing colors.

"Oh, I almost forgot." He jumped up and leaned over. Suddenly, they were surrounded by a circle of fairy lights.

"Walker, this is the most magical night ever."

"That's exactly what I wanted for you. A night off. Relaxation."

They sat and talked about everything except wedding plans. The conversation flowed as easily as the champagne. As they savored the last sips, she reached across and took his hand. "I don't ever want to leave. This night is perfection. I don't know how I got so lucky to find you."

"No, I'm the lucky one." He looked at her with so much love in his eyes that it took her breath away. He got up and walked around the table and pulled her to her feet, into his arms. As the last sliver of sun dipped below the horizon, he wrapped her snugly in his arms.

Aspen stood there, tucked up against Walker, trying to sear every detail of this night into her memory. The candles flickering in the slight breeze. The salty scent of the sea air mingling with the scent of the flowers. She turned her face up to him. "Thank you so much for this unbelievably thoughtful surprise. I love you so much and can't wait to be your wife."

"I can't wait for you to be my wife, too. I want you to be by my side forever."

"I hope when we're old and gray, and the many years have gone by, that we'll still pull out the memory of this night. And I'm sure I'll still feel the love you've shown me tonight." She nestled closer to him.

Walker stroked her hair as he held her close. "Just a little preview of how I plan on spending our next decades together, making you happy."

This moment could freeze in time as far as she was concerned. It was perfect. It was all she could ever ask for, and so much more.

And yet, there was still more to come. A lifetime of love ahead of them.

CHAPTER 23

Violet stood back, hands on hips, surveying the stone walkway that now led to the office porch. It had been backbreaking work in the Florida heat, but it had turned out just like she'd hoped. Every muscle in her body ached, but it was worth it.

Danny came up behind her and slowly began rubbing her sore shoulders. She leaned into his strong hands. He swept back her hair and kissed her neck. "Hard work, but it really did turn out nice, didn't it?"

"I couldn't have done it without your help." Everything. The walkway. The patio. How he'd helped her decorate all the cottages at Christmas. He'd become her rock, her friend, her helper. The one person she wanted to share everything with. She could hardly remember her life without him in it.

"I was just glad to get to have all this time with you."

She leaned back as he dropped his hands and kneaded her lower back. "That feels good."

"You did a lot of hard work this weekend."

"So did you." She turned around to face him and trailed a finger along his jawline. "I figured you'd be tired of my endless projects around here by now."

Danny shook his head and tucked a wayward lock of hair behind her ear. "I love seeing your visions for the cottages come to life."

"Thank you. But it does seem like I'm always thinking of something else that needs to be done." She looked up at him and brushed some dirt off his cheek.

The resort was coming together like she'd imagined it. They'd worked hard this last week putting in the walkway and a round stone patio in the courtyard. She'd wanted it all finished before Aspen's wedding, and with Danny's help, that had happened.

Danny pulled her into an embrace. "The resort does look remarkable."

Pride swept through her at his compliment, and she stood on tiptoe for a long, lingering kiss.

"Ah, hem."

She spun around at the sound of Robbie's voice. He grinned at her. "Don't stop on my account."

A blush rushed across her face, heating her cheeks. "Your timing is impeccable. You showed up right when the project was finished."

Rob eyed the new walkway and patio. "That looks like it was a lot of work. Guess I picked the right weekend to be out of town."

"Guess you did." Aspen rolled her eyes. But she knew Robbie would have helped if she'd asked.

"I'm glad you were here to help her, Danny."

"My pleasure."

"These really do make the place look even more remarkable than it did. You've done a great job here, Vi."

"Is this where I tell you I told you so? After all your negativity when I first bought the place?" she teased.

"You have to admit, the place was a dump when you bought it."

"Okay, I will admit that. But I had a vision." She grinned at her brother.

"Right. And no one should get between you and your plans." Rob laughed and turned to Danny. "But I really do truly appreciate all you do to help out Violet. You two make a good team."

"Is this also where I get to tell you I told you so?"

"Okay, I might not have been the biggest fan of you two dating, but Danny lived halfway across the state then. It seemed like your relationship was destined to fail."

"And yet, it didn't." Danny slipped his hand in hers.

Rob held up his hands. "Okay, I'll admit it. Vi was right, I was wrong. You two are really a great match."

Violet grinned, just barely stopping herself from sticking out her tongue like she had when they were kids. "Told you so."

Rob laughed. "Well, I should run. Just wanted to check in. If I don't see you before it, I'll see you at Aspen's wedding."

"Thanks for stopping by." She had to admit that praise from her big brother still felt really good.

Robbie left, and Danny pulled her back into his arms, kissing her gently. "I am glad to be here to help you. To just… spend time with you. I can't imagine not having you in my life."

She couldn't imagine not having Danny here in her life, either. Yes, he helped her with the resort, but it was so much more than that. He supported her decisions. Told her she was beautiful—not that she totally believed him. But he made her feel beautiful with just the way he looked at her.

"I'm ready for our next project together. And our next one. And the next. I want to always be here for you, Violet."

Her heart skipped a beat. *Always* be here for her?

"One of these days, we need to have a serious talk about our future." He kissed the side of her forehead and pulled her against him, holding her close.

Had he said *our* future? Her heart skipped another beat.

He let go of her and stepped back, tipping her chin up so she'd look right into his eyes. "I was going to wait until after Aspen's wedding. I know you're really busy right now."

She held her breath.

He took her hands in his. "But I want you in my life. Every day. Every minute. You've brought me such happiness. I should really wait until I have all this sorted out. Do some big gesture—and I promise I will. But I want to be certain we're on the same page." He paused and took a deep breath. "Violet, do you want to be with me, too? Like forever? Like—gosh, I should have been more prepared for this—do you think we should get married?"

She stared at him. Had he just... proposed?

"Look, I'm the worst at this ever. I should have bought a ring. Made a big deal. But after working with you all day today, being with you is so right. And... I just want to know. Will you marry me?"

Her heart hammered, and she reached up and touched his face. "Yes, I'll marry you. I can't imagine not having you in my life. And this is the perfect proposal. I don't need fancy things. A grand gesture, as you said. I just need... you."

"Okay, but just so you know, I *am* getting you a ring." He grinned. "And I am going to do a formal proposal thing. I just... got carried away. I was thinking about how much I love you, and love being with you, and wanted to share my life with you... I just... I had to ask."

She laughed. "And I love that about you." She kissed him again, knowing she'd remember this day forever. He could plan his grand gesture, but this was the day she'd remember as being when he asked her to marry him. When they decided to spend their lives together.

CHAPTER 24

Rose and Violet sat on the office porch having their coffee a few mornings before the wedding. "Your new walkway and patio look great," Rose said as she looked across the courtyard.

"Well, Danny was a big help."

"How are things going between you and Danny? It seems like you two are getting serious." Rose pinned Violet with a look, hoping Violet wouldn't avoid the question.

"We're doing fine..." A blush crept across Violet's face.

"Fine? What does that mean?" Rose eyed her again.

"He... he asked me to marry him."

"Well, that's wonderful." She glanced at Violet's hand.

"No. No ring yet. He kind of just… blurted it out. It was just so him. We'd had the best day together, even if it was hard work on the walkway. I just love doing projects with him. Spending time with him."

A wide grin spread across Rose's face. "A-ha. I knew it. The man is obviously smitten with you. I knew you two were getting serious."

"I'm madly in love with him and can't imagine my life without him." She grinned and shrugged. "He told Allison about proposing and she gave him so much trouble for not planning a big thing. He said he's going to do some kind of formal proposal, but I don't need that."

"I'm so happy for both of you."

Violet turned at the sound of someone approaching and her mouth dropped open. Rose spun around to see who it was.

"Mr. Murphy." Violet jumped up and hurried to greet him.

Rose sat shocked at seeing his face again. The man who had greeted her and Emmett each year when they checked into their cottage for their annual anniversary trip to Murphy's Place.

"Just Murphy. Please. That's what everyone calls me." Murphy swept his gaze around, pausing at each cottage, looking at the courtyard all planted with flowering bushes. Scattered chairs beckoned guests to come sit and relax. "It looks... different." He chortled. "Well, that's a real understatement."

"I made a few changes," Violet said.

"I'll say. It looks like a totally different place. I see you renamed it."

"I did. I hope that's okay. I just thought the place needed a fresh start."

"Hey, you bought it. It was yours to do what you wanted with it. Kinda like the new name. Would be strange to call it Murphy's since... well, you're not Murphy."

Rose stood and walked over beside Violet. "Murphy, it's good to see you."

He stared at Rose for a moment, then a spark of recognition flashed through his eyes. "Well, Mrs. Sherman. Wrong time of year for you to be here, isn't it? Don't you and the Mister come in September? Where is he?" He peered over to the porch.

That tweak to her heart caused her to pause for a moment. "My Emmett passed away last year. I came by myself to the cottages for our anniversary last September."

"I'm sorry. I didn't know." Murphy frowned, then snapped his fingers. "That reminds me. I had a letter I was supposed to give you on your anniversary. Didn't know the Mister wasn't going to be here, and that's why he sent it to me."

"A letter from Emmett?" Her heart started racing.

"It's in those old file boxes if you still have them. The ones in the back room."

Violet nodded quickly. "I have them. Shoved them into the storage closet. I haven't finished going through them. I'm the worst procrastinator on stuff like that."

"It's in the one with the year-end figures. That ledger I kept."

"Let me see if I can find it." Violet disappeared into the office.

"Come sit. I'll get you coffee while Violet is searching." Rose hurried in and returned with a mug of coffee, wondering if Violet would find the letter. And why had Emmett sent the letter here? Maybe an anniversary card?

Murphy took a sip. "Lot better than the coffee I served. Looks like Violet improved quite a lot around here. I admit, I finally just got tired of the upkeep and running the place. Was thrilled to finally find a buyer for it."

"Violet loves running the resort."

"So you came back for another visit, I guess."

"Actually, I've moved to Moonbeam. I needed a fresh start."

"Oh, I didn't know that. Well, I don't know much about what's happened in Moonbeam since I left. I guess I just need to run into the Jenkins twins so they can catch me up." He chuckled.

Violet returned and held out the envelope with a flourish. "I found it." She handed it to Rose.

"I think... I think I'll just take this back to my cottage and read it."

"You sure? You'll be okay?"

"I'll be fine. I'll check in with you later." She turned to Murphy. "And thank you for remembering this." She clasped the letter to her chest and turned and headed across the courtyard.

CHAPTER 25

Murphy leaned forward in his chair as Rose walked away. "So I wonder what's in that letter?"

"I don't know." Violet was a bit worried. Maybe she should have insisted on going with Rose. What if the letter upset her? But Rose was an independent woman these days and had made it clear she wanted to be alone.

"Wish I would have remembered about that letter back in September. He was pretty adamant Mrs. Sherman get it then. I just didn't understand why he sent it to me. That he... he wasn't going to be here."

"Well, she has it now. That's what's important." And hopefully Rose could handle whatever it said. Emmett's last letter about Pauline and Em had been a big enough shock.

Murphy stood. "Well, I don't want to keep you from your work. I just wanted to drop by and see the old place." He laughed. "It doesn't look so old anymore."

Violet reached out to stop him. "I don't think you should leave yet."

"Why not?"

"Because... because you can't. I mean, there's someone I think you'd like to meet. Let me pour you another cup of coffee and make a phone call."

Murphy's brow wrinkled, but he did as she said and sat back down.

Violet hurried inside to call Aspen. So many surprises today. But there was no way she was letting Murphy leave without seeing Aspen. Not since she'd heard Murphy was Aspen's uncle.

She grabbed her cell phone. "Aspen. You're never going to believe who just showed up here at the cottages."

"Who?"

"Murphy."

"My uncle?"

"One and the same. He's sitting out here on the front porch as we speak."

"I'll be right over."

Violet headed out with more coffee, wondering how this surprise meeting was going to work out...

Aspen clicked off the phone and let it drop onto the couch. She swallowed. Murphy was here. Right here. Right where she could meet him. Her uncle.

She hurried out of her cottage and headed to the office. She slowed when she got near the steps of the office porch. A man was sitting there chatting with Violet and drinking coffee. As if nothing momentous was happening.

Murphy. Her uncle. She squared her shoulders as she slowly climbed the stairs, then searched the man's face, looking for some family resemblance to Magnolia, but she didn't really see much.

The man stood as she approached, then frowned. "Oh, sorry. Didn't mean to stare. You just... remind me of... someone. Someone I used to know."

"You mean Magnolia?" The words just spilled out.

His eyes grew wide. "Yes, how did you know?"

"Magnolia was my mother."

"Was?" Pain flashed in his eyes. "Is she... gone?"

"Yes. She died last year."

"I'm so sorry. I didn't know." Murphy's features showed genuine sorrow.

Aspen shrugged. "I hadn't seen her in years. She left before I graduated high school."

Murphy shook his head. "Not surprising. She had a way of just up and disappearing. I haven't heard a word from her since she brought you to stay here at the cottages for a bit. You were just a little thing then. Maybe five, six or so? You stayed about a year and then one morning you were just gone. No goodbye. No thanks for letting us stay here for free. No note."

"Were we here when my dad came by looking for Magnolia?"

Murphy shook his head. "No, it was about a year after he came looking for her. I did try to call him after you two showed up. Figured he had a right to know. I knew Magnolia had done one of her disappearing acts on him but thought he had a right to see his daughter. But the number he left me was out of service."

"It was actually daughters. I have a sister. Magnolia gave her up for adoption."

"No kidding. She never said a word about that." Murphy shook his head. "My sister was certainly something, wasn't she?"

"She was," Aspen agreed.

Violet stood. "I'm going inside if you need me. I'll give you two time to talk." She slipped in the door.

"We could sit for a bit. Talk." Aspen motioned to the chairs.

Murphy nodded and settled back down on his seat. "So, how did you end up here in Moonbeam? At the cottages?"

"It's kind of a long story. But Magnolia sent a letter to me and to Willow—that's my sister—telling us to come to the cottages. Had a lawyer all set up for us to talk to. He was handling her estate. We found out Willow was my sister. Magnolia gave her up for adoption when she was about two. I can remember her from when I was a child. But Magnolia convinced me she was an imaginary friend. Eventually, the memories faded."

"But she kept you with her?" His brow furrowed.

She gave a little laugh. "Sort of. She had a

way of disappearing for weeks on end. Even when I was young."

"I'm sorry. I had no idea." He leaned forward. "Did your dad ever find you?"

"He did. It was just a few weeks ago. And Willow was here visiting. It was... quite the reunion."

"I'll bet. Bet he had a few choice words about my sister."

"He was heartbroken when Magnolia took us away. And she told me that Dad left us. Wasn't until we met with the lawyer that I found out it was the other way around."

"Sounds like Magnolia was trying to right some wrongs before she died. Make her peace."

"Maybe. But I am glad she sent those letters, and I found Willow. And Willow's husband hired a detective to track down Dad."

"How is your dad? I always thought he was a good guy. Magnolia was always harping at him. Nothing he did was good enough."

"I do remember them fighting a lot when I was little. But I do remember some times with Dad. Good times."

"I'm so sorry Magnolia did all this to you. To all of you. If I'd known, I would have tried to stop it. Not that anyone was ever able to stop her from doing what she set her mind to."

Murphy was nothing like she'd imagined. She'd thought he was all part of hiding her from her father. That he was in cahoots with Magnolia's plans. He hadn't even known about Willow.

"So, tell me all about you. About Willow. This is so unexpected to meet family after all these years."

"Well, I'm getting married in a week."

"No kidding. Well, congratulations. That's great news."

"Willow is coming. And Dad. He's going to walk me down the aisle." She looked over at him, an idea popping into her head. "Do you think you could stay? Come to the wedding? I know Dad would love to see you, and Willow will be so excited to meet you."

Murphy rubbed his chin and nodded. "I think that could be arranged."

"There's an opening here at the cottages. You could stay here." She frowned. "Or would that be strange for you? Staying at one of the cottages that used to be yours."

"No, I'd like that."

"Perfect. I can't believe I'm going to have all

this family at my wedding. It's something I never would have believed."

He reached over and patted her hand. "I can't think of anywhere I'd rather be. And I'm a bit tickled myself to have a family again. Magnolia was all the family I had, and when she disappeared? Then it was just me."

"Magnolia took a lot away from all of us."

"Guess you're pretty angry at her, huh?"

"I was. But I don't know. I seem to have made my peace with it. Now that Willow and Dad are back in my life." She smiled. "And you."

"You're a better person than I would be."

"I figure I can let the anger eat at me… or I can move on and enjoy the good things I have in my life now."

He smiled. "You're a good person, Aspen Caldwell."

"Thanks. I'm just trying to move past the hurt." She looked over at him and tilted her head. "So… what am I supposed to call you?"

"Uncle Murphy suits me just fine. My first name is… Ash. But no one calls me that."

"Ash—like the tree? The ash tree?"

"The very one."

"So that's where Magnolia got the idea to name us after trees."

He grinned. "Yep. And our mama's name was Cypress."

Laughter spilled out of her. "Seriously?"

"Yep."

"I guess it really is a family thing."

"So if you and your fella have kids, you going to keep up the tradition?"

"Not a chance." She shook her head. "The family tradition ends here."

"It's probably time to let that one die." He winked at her.

Aspen stood up. "How about you come inside and we'll get you all checked into a cottage."

He stood up beside her. "Sounds good. Guess I'll be out shopping for some nice clothes to wear to your wedding, too."

"And I've got to call Willow. She's going to be so excited. She'll be here tomorrow."

"Can't wait to meet her, either. Who knew I had two nieces?"

And who knew they'd finally all find their family again?

CHAPTER 26

R ose sat out on the deck of her cottage, holding Emmett's letter. She hadn't quite gotten up the nerve to open it yet. After Emmett's last letter where she found out he'd kept the secret about Pauline and helping her and Em out, she wasn't sure if she was ready for more surprises. Or ready to find out he'd kept any more secrets.

She ran her finger over his writing. The sprawling Rose written with his favorite fountain pen with his favorite dark charcoal gray ink. She closed her eyes as so many memories rushed past.

She finally opened her eyes and gingerly pried open the envelope. Tears sprang to her eyes as she saw his familiar handwriting.

. . .

My Dearest Rose,

I'm not sure I'm going to make it to our fiftieth wedding anniversary. But I have something special for you. I'm sending this letter for Murphy to give you if I'm not there…

Just know I love you deeply. Forever. Even after I'm gone.

But the most important thing I want you to know is… you must go out and live your life. Live life for me, my darling. Be the joyous, happy woman I know and love.

Find joy.

All my love,
  Emmett

PS. Go to our live oak tree. I've buried your surprise beneath it, right where we used to sit under it. Our special spot.

Rose swiped away the tears that rolled down her cheek. So like Emmett to make sure she had an anniversary gift. Even if she hadn't exactly gotten it on her anniversary.

She got up and went inside, setting the letter on the counter. She found a box of gardening supplies and pulled out a trowel. Prepared, she headed for the live oak tree on the edge of the Blue Heron Cottages property, right near the peach cottage where she and Emmett stayed each year.

She dropped to her knees, running her hand along the ground. How many hours had she and Emmett sat here talking? Making plans? Dreaming of how life would be for them. Not everything had turned out like they'd planned, of course. She'd never really thought about life without him. But here she was.

She stuck the trowel in the ground and began to dig. Right below the surface, she hit something. She dug around and then swept the sandy dirt away, revealing a metal box. She pulled it out, her heart racing as she slowly pried open the lid.

A small velvet bag rested inside. She loosened the string on it and opened it, raising it up and dumping out the contents into her hand. A smile spread across her lips when she saw the gift. "Oh, Emmett. It's perfect."

It was her beloved piece of sea glass, wrapped in thin strands of silver and hung on a silver chain. So that's what had happened to it. No wonder she couldn't find it in the move. She held it to her heart, feeling Emmett's love. Their love for each other. The wonderful life they'd had.

She undid the clasp and hooked the necklace around her neck, fingering the smooth glass. She pushed off the ground and walked down to the beach, standing at the water's edge.

She thought of going to tell Violet about the letter and showing her the surprise, but she just wanted to keep it to herself for a little bit. A few private moments with her memories. The ones she could take out and look at now without falling apart. She ran her finger over the sea glass again.

It didn't surprise her one bit that her blue heron swooped in and stood at the edge of the waves, joining her, looking at her.

A brilliant blue sky dotted with fluffy white clouds hung over the water. A gentle breeze blew in from the gulf. A perfect day. She looked out at the waves, constantly rolling to shore. Unending, just like her and Emmett's love.

But she was going to take his words to heart. Find joy. Live her life. Just like he'd asked.

CHAPTER 27

Aspen and Willow sat out in the courtyard the next evening. Their father and Murphy sat with them as they split a nice bottle of red wine.

Aspen noticed that Willow couldn't keep from looking back and forth between their father and their uncle. But she felt the same way. It was so surprising to have them both back in their lives. The father she thought had left her and the uncle she never knew she had. So much had changed for her this year.

Aspen turned at the sound of someone approaching, surprised to see Denise Wilkerson walking up to them. Denise waved. "Violet told me you were sitting out here."

Willow stood. "Denise, hi. What are you doing here?"

"Well, it seems that the legal issues were finally settled. I guess your lawyer got ahold of you?"

Aspen frowned. "No. I haven't heard from him."

"Me either," Willow added.

"I still don't agree with the decision, but the judge gave the majority of the inheritance to my siblings and me. I'm so sorry. But he did say that Magnolia's family deserved part of it. It's a pretty good sum." She held out a piece of legal-looking paper.

Willow reached for it and read it quickly, then handed it to Aspen. Aspen scanned it, stunned at the amount it showed for each of them. She looked up at Denise. "Really? This much?"

"Yes. But I know that Dad wanted you two to have all of it. I think Magnolia had explained what she did when she was younger. The mistakes she'd made. And he wanted to make her happy. Help her make amends for those mistakes. But this is how it worked out."

Willow looked over at Aspen. "I'm thinking that Aspen and I might set up a foundation. Use this money for worthy causes. What do you think, Aspen?"

"I know nothing about setting up foundations, but I think that's a wonderful idea," she said.

"Oh, I'd like to contribute, too." Denise nodded vigorously in agreement. "Father would be happy with that. Very happy."

"Are you girls certain that's what you want to do?" their father asked.

"Yes, this is exactly what I want to use the money for. Walker and I are happy just like we are. We don't need big sums of money. And... I don't really want the money from Magnolia. It won't make up for the past. For what she did. But... I'm over that now. I've made peace with it."

Willow reached out and squeezed her hand. "I'm glad you're making peace with your past."

"And I am glad she sent the letters, and I found out about Willow. And we eventually found you two." Aspen squared her shoulders and lifted her chin to look at each one of them in turn. "But this makes me happy. To think we can use the money to help make other people's lives easier. Maybe we could support the foster program. Or young mothers having a hard time raising kids on their own. That's what I'd love to do."

"Me too." Willow nodded vigorously. "That's a wonderful idea. Perfect."

"Well, I didn't mean to interrupt. I just wanted to make sure you were okay with how all this legal mess turned out. And let me know when you get the foundation set up. I'd love to help out." Denise smiled and started to step back.

"Denise, wait." Aspen jumped up. "You should stay. How would you like to come to my wedding this weekend? I feel like we're almost family."

Denise's eyes shone. "Yes, I'd love that." She grinned. "Would be nice to have siblings I'm not always arguing and disagreeing with."

"Perfect. It's Saturday. Six o'clock. Here at the cottages."

"I'll be here." Denise hugged her.

"We'll see you then."

Denise headed back across the courtyard, and Willow and Aspen sat back down.

"I think that's a fine thing you're doing setting up the foundation. I've got time on my hands now that I sold the cottages. And… I've been thinking of moving back to Moonbeam.

Didn't know how much I'd miss this place. Thinking of getting a small condo on the harbor where someone else does all the upkeep. So I'd love to help with the foundation." Murphy offered.

"Oh, I'd love for you to move here and be close. I can help you look for a place to live," Aspen offered.

"And we'd love help with the foundation," Willow added.

"You know, that's not a bad idea." Her father leaned forward in his chair, stroked his chin, and nodded. "There's no reason I need to stay way up north. I could make Moonbeam my home base." He laughed and his eyes twinkled with amusement. "You're going to have so much family near that you'll be sick of us."

"Never. I can't think of anything better than being surrounded by family." A family she never thought she'd have.

"Hey, now I'm jealous that we're not here," Willow said.

"But you're close and you can come visit whenever you want."

"Okay, but you'll be sick of me, too. I plan on visiting all the time." Her sister grinned.

"Doubt I could ever get sick of any of you."

Derek and Eli came walking up. Eli rushed over, his face flushed with excitement. He swung a bucket from hand to hand then held it up with a flourish for her to inspect. "Look, Aunt Aspen. Look at all the shells I found. Well, Dad found a few of them, but I found the bestest ones."

"You did a good job, Eli."

The boy's chest puffed up with pride, smiling from ear to ear. "I did do good, didn't I?"

Derek leaned down and kissed Willow, then placed his hand on her shoulder.

"Dad and I are going to wash them off, then I've got to take a shower." Eli scowled. "Don't wanna, but Dad says I have to before I go to bed."

"Your father is right." Willow began to stand.

"No, stay here and enjoy your family. I'll wrangle Eli into the shower. I'll send him out to kiss you good night before tucking him in," Derek said.

"You're the best."

Derek and Eli headed for their cottage. Aspen leaned back in her chair. Who would have thought when she arrived in Moonbeam with no money, no job, no place to live, that life would turn out like this?

Willow reached over and squeezed her hand. "Everything is pretty perfect, isn't it?"

"It is." Aspen looked up at the sky and swore for a moment she saw the silhouette of Magnolia's face in the clouds. She blinked, and it was gone.

CHAPTER 28

Aspen couldn't have asked for better weather for her wedding. The hot streak had broken last night when a storm came through. Today was sunny with a good breeze to chase away any humidity.

She glanced out at the courtyard where Violet, Willow, and Rose had set up everything. They'd chased her away when she offered to help, telling her to relax. How was she supposed to relax? She was getting married today!

She looked at the wedding dress for the hundredth time. It really was perfect. And it made her feel so close to Willow to be wearing the same dress she'd worn when she married Derek.

The door to her cottage opened and Willow walked in, already dressed. She looked lovely, and Aspen was half afraid that she'd look dowdy next to her beautiful sister.

"Okay, let's get ready," Willow said.

"Good, because I know you do hair better than I do." Willow did everything about makeup, hair, and clothes better than she did.

"Just sit back and relax. I've got this."

The time slipped by as Willow pulled Aspen's hair up and styled it with tendrils of curls hanging down. When her makeup was finished, Aspen stared in surprise. Although she knew Willow had put the makeup on, it didn't really look like she was wearing much. A bit of color on her eyelids. A hint of lipstick.

"Now we'll unzip the dress all the way so you can step into it. That way you won't muss your hair or makeup."

Willow helped her get the dress on and pulled up the long zipper in the back. She turned around slowly in front of the mirror, not believing this was really her. "Willow, you are a magician."

Willow laughed. "No, you're a beautiful woman all in your own right. You look lovely."

Aspen tried to see herself in a new light. Maybe Willow was right. She was always comparing herself with others and judging herself harshly in comparison. Maybe she could break that cycle. She did think she looked lovely in this dress with her hair all up and pretty.

She hugged her sister. "Thanks, Willow."

"Stand still," Tara commanded Walker.

"You sure are bossy." Walker yanked at his tie.

"You did a terrible job tying that. I'm doing it again. You want to look good, don't you?"

He didn't want to acknowledge his hands were shaking a bit, and that's why the tie had turned out lopsided. Tara deftly retied it, and he looked in the mirror, admitting it did look a lot better.

"There, you look pretty handsome, I do have to say."

"You don't look half bad yourself." Tara had settled on wearing black trousers and a blue silk blouse as her best man—best person, she insisted—outfit.

There was a knock at the door of the room he was getting ready in. "Walker, can we come in?" his mom called.

"Come on in, Mom."

Both of his parents came into the room. When his mother saw him, her eyes filled with tears.

"Now, now, dear. Don't start that. You have a long evening ahead of you." His father pulled out a handkerchief and handed it to her.

"But he looks so handsome. And Tara, that outfit is perfect. I can't believe my baby is getting married."

"Pretty sure I haven't been your baby for quite a few decades." Walker kissed his mom's cheek.

"You'll always be my baby."

And he knew that. No matter how old he got, if he was single or married, his mother would always consider him her baby. But over the years he'd gotten used to it, and—not that he'd tell her—didn't mind it a bit. He really had the best mom ever.

"There's quite the crowd out there," his father said. "Feels like most all the town is here."

"The Jenkins twins stopped me as they were walking to their seats and told me they knew you and Aspen were destined to be a couple from the first time they saw you two together." His mother smiled as she dried her tears.

"Who would ever argue with the Jenkins twins?" Walker laughed.

"I just wanted to see you before the ceremony starts. And tell you I love you. And that I'm so happy for you. Aspen is a wonderful woman. She is perfect for you. And I wish nothing but happiness for you two in the coming years." His mother hugged him.

"Thanks, Mom." He could hardly choke out the words. She had a way of saying things that got to his heart.

"We're going to go say hi to some people, then take our seats." She reached up and patted his cheek.

His parents headed out, and he turned and caught Tara blinking her eyes rapidly. "Ha, Mom got to you, too, didn't she?"

"I have no idea what you're talking about." She whirled around, walked over to the dresser, and fiddled with the comb and brush on it.

Another knock at the door and Violet poked her head in. "Ready for you to get to the arbor. We're almost ready to start."

"Come on, big brother, I'll show you the

way. Let's do this." Tara walked out the door and he followed, his heart jumping in his chest. He was finally going to get his wish. He was marrying the love of his life.

CHAPTER 29

V iolet and Rose came to Aspen's door. "How's it going in here?"

"We're almost ready. Oh, I almost forgot." Willow reached into her bag and pulled out a small box. "Something new."

Aspen opened the box and pulled out a thin silver bracelet. It had her and Willow's initials entwined on the band. "Oh, it's wonderful. That's so thoughtful. It's lovely."

"Just to remind you, I'm always with you. That we won't be separated again."

Aspen slipped it on her wrist, blinking back tears.

Rose stepped forward. "Then this is perfect. I have something you can borrow...and it's blue." She slipped off the necklace she was wearing. "My Emmett had this made for me. It's from a piece of sea glass we found on our honeymoon."

"Oh, Rose. I love it. And look, it matches the ribbons in my flowers." Aspen spun around. "Can you put it on me?"

Rose latched the necklace, and Aspen turned to look in the mirror. "It's just perfect. And it means so much to me that you loaned it to me."

Violet peeked out the window. "Looks like they're almost ready to begin. Come on, Rose. Let's take our seats."

Violet and Rose slipped out the door. Aspen walked over to the window and looked out, gasping as she saw all the people seated in the chairs. "Willow, come look."

Willow crossed over to look out the window, then laughed. "And you thought there would be no one sitting on your side of the wedding."

"That's half of Walker's family sitting on the bride's side. Look, even his mother and father."

"And you have Dad, Uncle Murphy, Derek, Eli, Violet, Rose, and look, there's Denise, too. And... well, look at all your friends out there."

Music started to play. The song she'd picked to walk down the aisle—with Willow's help, of course. And now she was just so grateful for all of her sister's help.

Her father knocked at the door and stepped inside. A wide grin spread across his features. "Oh, Aspen. You look beautiful. So beautiful."

"Thanks, Dad."

"Are you ready, honey?"

She nodded and took his arm. Willow headed out first and walked down the aisle. Her dad led her over to the start of the aisle lined with flowers.

Walker looked up and saw her, and the look of love in his eyes caused her heart to flutter. Tears threatened the corners of her eyes. But she wasn't going to cry. She wasn't.

She nodded to her father, and they began to walk. She was walking down the aisle with her *father*. She would never have believed that, even just a few weeks ago. When they reached the arbor, her dad placed her hand in Walker's, kissed her cheek, and went to sit by Murphy.

Walker leaned forward and whispered, "You're the most beautiful woman I've ever seen. Can't wait to marry you."

She squeezed his hand as her heart soared in her chest and a peace settled over her replacing her nervousness about the ceremony. The pastor spoke, and they said their vows. It all passed in a blur for her. All she knew was Walker was right there with her. Where he belonged. Where she belonged.

"You may kiss the bride."

A wide grin spread across Walker's face, then he leaned down and kissed her, lingering on her lips as he wrapped his arms around her. The crowd started clapping, and she blushed as she stepped back.

"I give you Aspen and Walker Bodine," the pastor announced.

They stood by the arbor and she ran her gaze around all their friends and family gathered to celebrate with them. Happiness swelled through her.

And those tears she promised not to shed refused to listen and ran down her cheeks. Walker looked at her, smiled, and brushed them away with his thumb.

He took her hand in his as they walked back down the aisle. He paused at the end of it and pulled her back into his arms. "I've never been happier, Mrs. Bodine."

"I haven't either." She kissed him, savoring the moment, knowing she was right where she belonged.

CHAPTER 30

The reception lingered on, long after the sun set. Violet had placed lanterns all around the edges of the courtyard and strung white lights across, so the whole area was lit with a warm glow.

She'd thanked Violet a million times for letting them use the courtyard for the wedding until Violet laughed and told her no more thanks. But it really did look beautiful. And more perfect than she'd ever imagined for her wedding.

Walker's parents walked up to where Walker and Aspen were standing. "It was really a lovely ceremony, wasn't it?" Mrs. Bodine said.

"I think so. And Violet, Rose, and Willow

outdid themselves decorating the courtyard. I can't imagine a more perfect wedding." Aspen leaned against Walker as he tightened his arm around her. "And Mrs. Bodine, you and Mr. Bodine sat on the bride's side during the ceremony. I was so surprised. And... pleased."

"Ah, that's because you're our daughter now. There are no sides. Just one big family."

Aspen held back the tears that chased the corners of her eyes yet again.

"Also, one more thing. It's about time you stop with the Mr. and Mrs. Bodine. You can call us Sally and Jimmy."

"Thank you, Sally." She tried the name on for size. It felt wonderful. Like she was truly part of the family.

"And another thing," Jimmy added. "We heard how you decided to create the foundation with the money you inherited from your mother. That was very generous."

"I just felt like it was the right thing to do." And Walker had been very agreeable too, even though it meant the two of them wouldn't have the money to spend. But they were happy how they were. They didn't need large sums of money to be happy.

"Well, Sally and I thought of the perfect wedding present for you two. We think it's the right thing to do to give you this." Jimmy held out a key.

"What's that, Dad?" Walker eyed his father.

"It's a key to your Uncle Darrell's house on the harbor. He moved into that retirement place with your aunt. Didn't want the upkeep of the house. But it's been in the family for generations. So he and I struck a deal. And I'd like you and Aspen to have it."

"If you want it," Sally added.

Aspen looked up at Walker, bewildered. His parents were giving them a *house?*

"Dad, that's much too generous."

"No, it's not. It's family property. And you— both of you—are family."

Walker looked down at her. "It is a nice place. Right on the harbor. Four bedrooms, three baths, and a wonderful covered porch overlooking the harbor."

"It's not far from our home, but far enough that you two newlyweds can have your privacy." Sally gave them a knowing smile. "So, what do you say? Say, yes."

Aspen shared a long look with Walker,

overwhelmed with joy at how her life was falling into place. She nodded and Walker turned to his parents. "We say thank you." He hugged his mom and then his dad.

Sally opened her arms and Aspen walked into them, feeling loved and accepted. Sally whispered in her ear, "I just want you to know that you can also call me Mom… if you want to, of course."

Tears sprang to Aspen's eyes, and she clung to Sally. "I'd… I'd like that."

"Perfect. I'd like that too. I'd love another daughter."

Sally wouldn't replace Magnolia, of course. Those memories and the tough times she'd had with Magnolia would always be there. But being a part of the Bodines? And Sally asking her to call her Mom? It truly felt like family.

Her dad, Willow, and Derek walked up. Murphy wasn't far behind them, with Eli scampering at his side, holding his hand.

"What's all this hugging going on? Aspen, are you crying?" Her father came over and placed his hand on her shoulder. "You okay?"

"I'm perfect. I've never been better. These are happy tears. I'm here surrounded by my family. Something I never knew I wanted so badly or needed so much. And here you all are."

Walker leaned down, kissed her forehead, and whispered, "Our own family of two, and our huge family of all of these people we love."

CHAPTER 31

"Rose, I've been meaning to ask you something." George sat next to her the next evening as they sat out on the beach watching the sunset.

"What's that?"

"I was wondering. I mean, we go out to eat a lot. Do things together. Do you think..." He paused, deep furrows between his brows. "Do you think those are... dates?"

"What? No. I'm not ready to date. Not yet."

He relaxed in his chair and gave her a smile. "Okay, good. We're just hanging out as friends. Because I ran into the twins and they said something about us dating. And I thought... I thought we were just doing things together. As friends. But then I wasn't sure how you thought of everything." He laughed. "Those Jenkins twins sure got me confused."

"Well, we won't let the twins define who we are. What we're doing." Rose smiled at him. "We're just friends. Good friends."

"That's fine with me." He reached over and briefly squeezed her hand. "You've been a very good friend to me. And I enjoy having someone to do things with. Go out to eat with. Go to the movies. And I really loved going antiquing with you the other day."

"Not to mention watching the sunsets. It's nice to have company while I sit here watching them." Rose looked over at George, her heart full of emotion. "So… it's okay with you? That we just stay friends. At least… for now."

"It's fine with me. I just wasn't certain if you thought we should be officially dating or something like that. We do spend a lot of time together."

"I think we can be what we want to be. And I enjoy spending time with you. I'm just not ready for it to be something more. Emmett's only been gone…" She frowned. "I guess it's been over a year and a half now."

"But he's still there in your thoughts all the time, isn't he?"

"He is."

"My Becky is in mine a lot, too. She always will be."

"But Emmett, in his last letter to me, he told me to go find joy. And that's what I plan to do." She took George's hand in hers, the warmth of his fingers spreading through her. "And you do bring me joy."

"And you, me." George pulled her hands to his lips and kissed them.

They sat there like that, enjoying the sunset. Enjoying each other. And Rose was certain her future was bright now. Certain she'd find joy. She'd already found it here in Moonbeam.

I hope you enjoyed the Blue Heron Cottages series. From the bottom of my heart, I want to extend my deepest thanks and gratitude to each of you who journeyed through this series with me.

If you missed it, the Moonbeam Bay series is set in the same story world. You can find all of my books and the official reading order here on my website. The next series is Magnolia Key, coming in spring of 2024.

Each time I sit down to write, I'm reminded of all of you who have embraced my stories of love and community. I hope you've found a bit of home in these pages.

I'm eternally grateful for each and every one of you.

With much love, Kay

ALSO BY KAY CORRELL

COMFORT CROSSING ~ THE SERIES

The Shop on Main - Book One

The Memory Box - Book Two

The Christmas Cottage - A Holiday Novella (Book 2.5)

The Letter - Book Three

The Christmas Scarf - A Holiday Novella (Book 3.5)

The Magnolia Cafe - Book Four

The Unexpected Wedding - Book Five

The Wedding in the Grove (crossover short story between series - Josephine and Paul from The Letter.)

LIGHTHOUSE POINT ~ THE SERIES

Wish Upon a Shell - Book One

Wedding on the Beach - Book Two

Love at the Lighthouse - Book Three

Cottage near the Point - Book Four

Return to the Island - Book Five

Bungalow by the Bay - Book Six

Christmas Comes to Lighthouse Point - Book Seven

CHARMING INN ~ Return to Lighthouse Point

One Simple Wish - Book One

Two of a Kind - Book Two

Three Little Things - Book Three

Four Short Weeks - Book Four

Five Years or So - Book Five

Six Hours Away - Book Six

Charming Christmas - Book Seven

SWEET RIVER ~ THE SERIES

A Dream to Believe in - Book One

A Memory to Cherish - Book Two

A Song to Remember - Book Three

A Time to Forgive - Book Four

A Summer of Secrets - Book Five

A Moment in the Moonlight - Book Six

MOONBEAM BAY ~ THE SERIES

The Parker Women - Book One

The Parker Cafe - Book Two

A Heather Parker Original - Book Three

The Parker Family Secret - Book Four

Grace Parker's Peach Pie - Book Five

The Perks of Being a Parker - Book Six

BLUE HERON COTTAGES ~ THE SERIES

Memories of the Beach - Book One

Walks along the Shore - Book Two

Bookshop near the Coast - Book Three

Restaurant on the Wharf - Book Four

Lilacs by the Sea - Book Five

Flower Shop on Magnolia - Book Six

Christmas by the Bay - Book Seven

Sea Glass from the Past - Book Eight

WIND CHIME BEACH ~ A stand-alone novel

INDIGO BAY ~

Sweet Days by the Bay - Kay's complete collection of stories in the Indigo Bay series

ABOUT THE AUTHOR

Kay Correll is a USA Today bestselling author of sweet, heartwarming stories that are a cross between women's fiction and contemporary romance. She is known for her charming small towns, quirky townsfolk, and the enduring strong friendships between the women in her books.

Kay splits her time between the southwest coast of Florida and the Midwest of the U.S. and can often be found out and about with her camera, taking a myriad of photographs, often incorporating them into her book covers. When not lost in her writing or photography, she can be found spending time with her ever-supportive husband, knitting, or playing with her puppies - a cavalier who is too cute for his own good and a naughty but adorable Australian shepherd. Their five boys are all grown now and while she misses the rowdy boy-noise chaos, she is thoroughly enjoying her empty nest years.

Learn more about Kay and her books at
kaycorrell.com

While you're there, sign up for her newsletter to
hear about new releases, sales, and giveaways.

WHERE TO FIND ME:
My shop: shop.kaycorrell.com
My author website: kaycorrell.com
authorcontact@kaycorrell.com

Join my Facebook Reader Group. We have lots
of fun and you'll hear about sales and new
releases first!
www.facebook.com/groups/KayCorrell/

I love to hear from my readers. Feel free to
contact me at authorcontact@kaycorrell.com

facebook.com/KayCorrellAuthor

instagram.com/kaycorrell

pinterest.com/kaycorrellauthor

amazon.com/author/kaycorrell

bookbub.com/authors/kay-correll

Printed in the USA
CPSIA information can be obtained
at www.ICGtesting.com
LVHW041143300124
770177LV00003B/644